A ~~Winter in Whistler~~

A winter in Whistler they'll never forget...

Family-run Cobalt Lake Resort is Whistler's most exclusive winter destination, but the past few Christmas seasons have seen little festive spirit following the tragic passing of the family matriarch.

But this year owner Brad Daniels and his daughter, Cassandra, are determined to recapture the holiday magic. And when two familiar faces from their pasts come calling, it's soon more than just the cold and snow that's making them shiver...

Read Brad and Faith's story in:
The Billionaire's Festive Reunion
By Cara Colter

Read Cassandra and Rayce's story in:
Their Midnight Mistletoe Kiss
By Michele Renae

Dear Reader,

This was a fun story to write! And what made it even more enjoyable was working with Cara Colter to create the Daniels family and the Cobalt Lake Resort. Cara, who hails from British Columbia, gets all the credit for her knowledge on Whistler and skiing; I've never skied, but having lived in Minnesota all my life, I figure I got the winter stuff right.

This is the first Christmas story I've written for Harlequin, and I simply had to incorporate some of my holiday favorites. I always put a part of myself into my stories, but I'll never reveal those personal touches!

This A White Christmas in Whistler duet starts with Cara's story, which features a billionaire dad, a widower who gets a second chance to romance his high school sweetheart. To continue with the high school theme, I've matched a wounded Olympic athlete with his unrequited high school crush.

Here's to a happy holiday filled with warm and wondrous family love!

Michele

THEIR MIDNIGHT
MISTLETOE KISS

MICHELE RENAE

ROMANCE

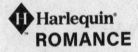

Harlequin® ROMANCE

ISBN-13: 978-1-335-21614-4

Their Midnight Mistletoe Kiss

Copyright © 2024 by Michele Hauf

Harlequin Enterprises ULC
22 Adelaide St. West, 41st Floor
Toronto, Ontario M5H 4E3, Canada
www.Harlequin.com

Printed in U.S.A.

Michele Renae is the pseudonym for award-winning author Michele Hauf. She has published over ninety novels in historical, paranormal and contemporary romance and fantasy, as well as written action/adventure as Alex Archer. Instead of "writing what she knows," she prefers to write "what she would love to know and do" (and yes, that includes being a jewel thief and/or a brain surgeon).

You can email Michele at toastfaery@gmail.com. Instagram: @MicheleHauf
Pinterest: @toastfaery

Books by Michele Renae

Harlequin Romance

If the Fairy Tale Fits...

Cinderella's Billion-Dollar Invitation

Cinderella's Second Chance in Paris
The CEO and the Single Dad
Parisian Escape with the Billionaire
Consequence of Their Parisian Night
Two Week Temptation in Paradise

Visit the Author Profile page
at Harlequin.com.

To everyone who has tasted snowflakes and engaged in snowball fights filled with laughter. And if you haven't—what are you waiting for?

Praise for
Michele Renae

CHAPTER ONE

CASSANDRA DANIELS SNAPPED photographs of the massive floral display in the Cobalt Lake Resort lobby. It had been delivered an hour earlier and it had taken two delivery men to carry in the heavy vase overflowing with white and red poinsettia, deep red roses, sprays of glittered baby's breath, and sprigs of wispy greens. A plush red velvet ribbon wove in and around the bouquet.

"Marvelous." She studied the few shots and then color-adjusted her favorite to post on the resort's social media feed. "Mom would be pleased."

In fact, her mother, Cynthia Daniels, would only employ her approving "marvelous" when something was worthy of praise. Be it decorations around the resort, a chef's special dinner or even the sound of boots crunching fresh-fallen snow on a peaceful Christmas morning.

With a heavy sigh, Cassandra's shoulders dropped. It had been two years since her mother's death. An avalanche while she was out skiing had taken her from this world much too early. Grief still teased at Cassandra and seemed to attack at the most unexpected moments. Tears in front of the guests? Never. She could hold them back until she retreated to her apartment. Yet the invisible emotional tears in her heart seemed never-ending.

Christmas had been her mom's favorite season. As the resort manager, Cynthia Daniels had taken seriously the task of decorating for Christmas. Each year she employed a crew of temporary workers for a week to make it all come together. From the guest rooms to the lobby, the spa, the exterior and all through the outer areas, including the cozy wooden walkway that curled around the lake. Not a patch of property remained untouched by the festive spirit.

Last year Cassandra hadn't been able to summon the spirit necessary to put up more than some interior garlands and ribbons. Her heart had felt the lack of her mother's presence in those missing decorations. This year she was determined to pull herself up from the grief, rediscover her own joy and create a Christmas that would make her mother declare, "Marvelous."

The outdoor decorating had been completed by a local crew. The trees were kept strung with lights throughout the year, as well as the lake walk. Inside the resort everything sparkled, glimmered and danced with sugarplums, tidy presents, tiny snowmen and snow-sprinkled figurines, poinsettias, holly and the requisite mistletoe. The spicy aroma of cinnamon and nutmeg greeted guests in the lobby. Each guest room was subtly touched with Christmas. And the last of the ornaments were currently being placed on the twenty-eight-foot blue spruce that greeted guests as they entered the lobby.

Cassandra heard someone call her name. One of the night maids had begged to help with decorations because *Christmas was her jam*, and she'd stayed on this morning to help.

"It's finished," Kay announced with a gleeful clap and a Vanna White–like splay of her hand toward the massive tree.

"It looks amazing," Cassandra enthused.

She strolled toward the tree, her eyes moving up, down and around to take it in. She'd given exact instructions on how the decorations should be hung. The ribbons strung evenly, yet artfully. Tinsel used sparely. No two similar ornaments close together. The red glass ornaments hung equal distances apart…

Yes, she was aware of her need for perfection. But Cassandra never asked for more than was possible. And if she did notice something out of place she'd never call out an employee for what wasn't a mistake but rather a misplacement. Her dad had once let her in on the backroom talk that the employees thought she could be demanding but they didn't mind because she countered it with kindness and respect.

Kindness was never difficult. It should be a person's normal mode; that's what her mom had taught her. And if you put out a warm welcoming vibe, it would return to you in greater amounts.

With a touch to a handblown glass sleigh that she remembered her dad giving her a few Christmases earlier, she then trailed her fingers over the shimmery silver tinsel. Astringent pine filled her nostrils. The ever-present scent of burning cedar emanated from the fireplace opposite the tree. Nearby a trio of peppermint candles sweetened the air. Cap that with the cinnamon sticks hung here and there within the pine boughs. The delicious perfume epitomized Christmas.

Cassandra stood back, hands on her hips. The tree looked Instagram-worthy. More photos were necessary! Could this mean she was almost finished with decorating? Save a few smaller tasks she had on her list—

"Wait." Her eyes darted over the tree hung with ornaments the Daniels family had collected over the twenty-eight years her parents had been married. She didn't see it. The one ornament she'd requested Kay take special care in hanging front and center. "Kay?"

"Yes, Miss Daniels?"

She loved Kay like an aunt who tended to smile at her and then sneak up close to tuck in a stray tag or remove a bit of lint from her sweater. Just as fussy about some things as Cassandra could be.

"Where is the ornament I told you about? It was my mom's favorite ornament. I made it for her when I was eight."

"I didn't see the ornament you described. A wood star?"

"Yes, a star made from twigs I collected in the forest. I glued them together. In the center was a photo of me and my mom. It gets front and center placement every year. It had to have been with the other ornaments. Did you check?"

"The bins are over there." Kay pointed to a rolling cart stacked neatly with clear plastic storage bins. All of them empty. "The boys brought in all the bins labeled for Christmas yesterday evening. Should I send them back to the storage room to check for more?"

"Of course. Or no, I'll do it." They'd done their part. Besides, she was the best person to recognize the missing item.

"This is not right. It's… It can't be Christmas," she said, her voice wavering. The courage she'd summoned to step away from the grief over the loss of her mother began to falter. Her stomach clenched. "Not without that ornament."

She noticed someone near the wall behind the tree bend down. "No!"

The employee who held the light switch box connected to the tree froze, half bent over. He flicked Cassandra a wondering look.

"No light! Not until it's perfect," she said, a bit too loudly. She sucked in her lower lip.

"But shouldn't we check to see that they work?" the startled man asked of her.

Cassandra shook her head adamantly. "Not until the ornament is in place. I'll look for it. You can clean up and return the bins to the storage room. But no one turns on the lights until you get the go-ahead from me. Understand?"

The half dozen employees standing around muttered their agreement.

Cassandra gave her sweater hem a commanding tug and nodded. Christmas simply would not happen until that ornament held the place of honor on the tree.

Someone seemed very agitated about a missing ornament.

Rayce Ryan observed the commotion in the resort lobby. No one had seen him enter, though that was by choice, given he purposely stood near a frothy display of pine, ribbons and sparkly snowflakes; Christmas camouflage. The entire three-story open lobby was decorated to the nines with red, green, sparkles, snowflakes, wreathes—it even smelled like Christmas.

It had been a long time since he'd celebrated Christmas with family. Memories of cozy flannel pajamas, hot chocolates by the fire and opening presents leaped to his mind and gave him a rare genuine smile. He'd had a great childhood. But when he hit his teen years, life had changed in so many ways. Most of it good. The worst of it? He'd lost the only family he'd ever known.

Might he dream to someday have family again? And along with that, a real home?

Some dreams were impossible. Besides, he'd once had the sweet life. A guy had no right to complain. Even as broken as he was. Rayce had begun to make a new life for himself. To perhaps capture a bit of that sweet life again. And it started here at Cobalt Lake Resort.

Rayce veered his attention back to the lobby. Something wasn't right. And it seemed to circle around the petite blonde wearing a white sweater and slacks. Her hair was silver-white as well. Visions of sugar pixies danced in his head. Er, no, it was plums or snow princesses—he always got his song lyrics confused.

With a swelling of his heart, he suddenly recognized the pale beauty. It had been years since he'd last seen her, but he'd thought of her often in the interim. That she seemed upset by a missing ornament didn't surprise him. She'd always been—what did they call it—type A? Or more appropriately *driven*, as he'd once labeled her.

"Driven and unobtainable," he muttered.

Another grin stretched his travel-weary jaw. His flight from Florida had been delayed, turbulent, noisy—two crying babies—and alcohol-free. It was mid-afternoon and he was ready for a nap. Or a beer. Probably both. As an Alpine ski racer, he'd once thrived on six hours of sleep and eighteen hours of training, skiing and partying. Now? Life had decided to shove him on his face. Hard. And he was still recovering.

After the snow princess commanded to those standing around the Christmas tree that there was to be no light, she then grabbed a clipboard and turned to look right at him. The recognition on her face was a mix of surprise, curiosity and…disappointment?

A look with which Rayce had become all too familiar. Had *everyone* watched his colossal crash when he'd lost an edge at top speed on the giant slalom at last year's winter Olympics? Well, if they hadn't, they'd likely seen memes of it on social media. His most immense failure endlessly repeated and looped, and even set to farcical music. All because he'd been betrayed by a woman he loved.

Stupid heart.

No, he couldn't be reading the snow princess's expression right. She was involved in taking care of business. Ever busy. Always on the go. Always out of reach.

He waved. She had to know he was due to arrive today. He'd dealt with her dad, Brad Daniels, throughout the hiring process. The man had picked him up from the airport. They had chatted about their hopes for good ski conditions and that Rayce would have to establish his own teaching schedule. Brad had dropped him off with apologies because he'd had to return to town to pick up some parts for one of their snow machines.

Left to himself to figure things out? Not an issue. Rayce was a self-starter and could pick up anything on the fly. This should be an easy gig. Thanks to far too many years of training, he was disciplined as hell. But while his body was in the program no matter the challenges presented, it was his heart that usually ended up bringing him down.

Thus, his reason for standing here in the Cobalt Lake Resort. He'd been hired for the season as their guest ski instructor. Like it or not.

He hadn't decided if he did like it or not. The

experience would reacclimate him to the slopes. And, with hope, allow him to start over. To figure out his next step. To…be a normal person for once in his life. Not some guy who had devoted over fifteen years of his life to training, competing, media appearances and giving 200 percent, including blood and sweat. And most of those years without family to keep him grounded and remind him that he was loved.

Rayce missed his grandparents. Was there anyone out there who could show him the immense love and kindness Roger and Elaine Ryan had? If there was, he desperately wanted to swerve in their direction.

With a nod toward Cassandra, he grabbed his suitcase and rolled it toward her, even as she started walking away from him while gesturing that he follow. He remembered her well. They'd attended the same high school in Whistler. He'd been a jock; she'd been all brains and academic achievement. She had been The One He Could Never Have.

He knew because he'd tried. And failed.

But did that mean he had to give up on the dream? No, Rayce Ryan never gave up—until the task injured him so badly he had no choice but to bow out.

Cassandra looked as beautiful as ever. Probably even prettier because she'd done something with her hair; it was snow-white instead of the sunny blonde she'd once been. Her mouth was soft pink. And the sway of her hair with each of her strides, the way it dusted her elbows...

Rayce knew his heartbeats weren't skipping from exertion right now.

"Rayce Ryan!" She paused and turned to shake his hand. "Dad must have just dropped you off?"

"He did, with instructions to take the place in and get comfortable. I know the slopes. I did spend every winter here my entire childhood."

"Right. How many times did my dad have to send out security to rein you in after midnight?"

"Too many to count." He chuckled. "You can't keep a ski bum off the powder."

"No, you can't. But I think you should claim professional over bum."

"Eh. I'll always be a bum, living for the fresh pow and carving my line through the corduroy."

She smiled but caught her mirth quickly and adjusted her mouth to a tight line. "We've set up security cameras now. Just a warning if you have any midnight black runs planned. It's for the safety of our guests. Is that your only baggage?"

"I left my skis and equipment in the side entry where your dad let me off."

"Perfect. You can claim an employee locker later; that should fit most of your gear. If you'll walk with me." She strolled past the reception desk and down a long hallway. What a sensual sway to those slender hips. The woman was obviously a skier. She knew how to move. "I'm a bit busy right now," she called over her shoulder.

Her wavy hair bounced, enticing him to catch up and consider touching it. Admiration from a distance had been about all he'd managed with Cassandra Daniels. Yet seeing her again after nearly ten years did inspire him to wonder if he could broach that distance. Walk alongside those swaying hips that reminded him of a skier's schuss down the slopes.

"I'll get you to your cabin and leave you to take the place in on your own," she continued. "You're familiar with the layout of the resort. Not much has changed since our teen days, though we did add another lift and the outdoor amenities have doubled. Do you have a schedule prepared for next week?"

"Not yet. Your dad said I could take a few days to familiarize myself with the slopes and figure out my schedule for private lessons."

The look she cast over her shoulder judged him nine ways up and down. Rayce was used to that look. From everyone. Often it was accompanied by expectation. Everyone demanded so much from an Olympic athlete.

And he had let everyone down.

With an assessing nod, she finally said, "In a

few days I'll touch base with you and get your schedule entered into the database."

Cassandra pushed open an outer door and barely broke stride as she took off down a heated sidewalk that curved around the backside of a high snow-frosted hedgerow. It was only ten degrees today, but she didn't flinch from the chill. Rayce, on the other hand, had grown accustomed to the Florida weather over the past year he'd spent in recovery. Jet Skiing and scuba diving warmed a man's soul in ways a frigid Canadian winter never could.

"This is the employee route," she said over a shoulder. "You're welcome to walk through the guest area, but it's quicker and more efficient this way."

"I suspect efficiency is your superpower."

Another judging glance. Or was it curiosity this time?

The woman had changed little since high school. Still pretty, still put together when it came to clothing and makeup. Still holding her head a level above all others. Because she was smart, or because she felt entitled? Had to be the smarts. The Daniels family had owned this resort since he could remember and held a trusted place in the Whistler community.

As Rayce followed her sure stride, he couldn't resist wondering if he might wiggle under her skin, nudge the snow princess off her throne to see if there was a warm, caring individual underneath the stoicism.

What the heck, man? His heart was interfering far too early. *Keep your eyes off her hips.*

"I mean," he corrected his comment about her superpower, "from what I remember about our high school days. You were driven."

"And you were a star." She marched up half a dozen wood steps to a small cabin capped with an A-frame roof and a frosting of pristine snow. She tapped a digital code into the box by the door. "Here's your new home away from home. The code is 5489. That's your code for all entries around the resort. It's written down in the welcome materials inside."

A home away from home? Rayce hadn't labeled a domicile *home* in—it had been since he'd left his grandparents' house to travel the racing circuit. Since then, hotels, airports and the occasional couch had served as shelter. This cabin was merely another place to sleep and eat while life tried its hand at him.

Cassandra pulled open the door and he walked up. Before crossing the threshold, he stopped and when he tried to meet her gaze, she suddenly seemed nervous, avoiding eye contact and pushing her hair over one ear.

"Are you...okay with me working here?" he asked.

Her pale blue eyes darted between his, speculating, perhaps even making decisions that only the female species made; things he could never comprehend. Her soft pink lips parted in wonder. "Whyever wouldn't I be?"

He shrugged. Because he recalled her walking away from him once. It had been ten years ago. They had been teenagers. Surrounded by friends and anyone who mattered in their lives. Oddly, that moment still hurt his heart. Rejection proved a more brutal wound than failure could ever inflict.

"The Cobalt Lake Resort is excited to feature Rayce Ryan as our exclusive ski professional this season," she said, or rather recited like some kind of marketing promotion.

"But what about you?" he tried. "Are you... excited?"

"I...I'm pleased you're here?"

"Are you asking me or telling yourself?"

"I don't understand the question." She checked her watch. "I really hate to leave you, but I need to get back to the task at hand."

"Something about an ornament?" That didn't sound so pressing, but what did he know?

"Exactly."

She offered her hand to shake, which he did. Despite the frigid temperature, her skin was warm, and it allowed him a few more seconds to stand in her atmosphere. Take in her beauty. And wonder about the thoughts that were bouncing around inside her head. What did she think of him? Dumb jock? Handsome not-so-strange stranger? Just another employee? Failed Olympian?

Her phone rang and she checked the screen.

"That's my dad. I'll catch up with you later, Mr. Ryan. You have free run of the resort. But do alert security to get an employee badge before you head off to a slope. The GPS in the badge constantly pings the security office, so if there's ever an accident…"

"Will do."

And then she was off, as quickly and efficiently as was possible, the phone pressed to her ear as she chatted with her dad. The moment was so—

Déjà vu struck Rayce with stunning precision. She'd run away from him during the high school dance. After he'd bent to kiss her. In that one precious moment when the world had stopped and his heart had leaped for the stars.

And he had fallen.

Running his fingers through his hair, he watched until Cassandra disappeared beyond the hedges.

"She's going to disturb your heart again, dude."

Or maybe, she'd never stopped.

CHAPTER TWO

"I KNOW, but that ornament means so much to me," Cassandra said to her dad, who had called from the parts supplier in town to see if she needed him to pick up anything. She'd mentioned that the tree was almost ready to be lit. Almost.

"Cassie, the tree is the big welcome to the resort. We have to turn on the lights."

"Just let me find the ornament first. Please? It won't take long. Give me a few days to comb through the resort?"

His sigh reminded her that they'd been through a lot these past few years. He'd been there with an arm around her shoulder and a kiss to the top of her head whenever she'd felt her lower lip wobbling and the memory of her mother emerge. He had gone through the same grief but remarkably had recently been able to welcome his high school girlfriend, Faith, back into his life after thirty years apart. They'd just announced their engagement.

"I'll give you a week," he said. "But that's far too long to allow the tree to sit there dark."

"I promise I'll find it sooner." And now to change the subject… "Can you pick up some of those monster cinnamon rolls from the bakery for me? I know you're going to make a stop there."

"I do love those cinnamon rolls." Despite the Daniels family's love for health and fitness, they were a favorite treat. Who could resist that gooey, sweet cream cheese frosting? "Oh, did you run into Rayce Ryan?"

"Yes, I gave him a quick lay of the land and showed him to his cabin."

"Take care of him, Cassie. He's going to attract new business as our resident ski professional. And the guy's a looker, eh?"

"Oh, Dad, I think I hear a cinnamon roll calling for you. Talk to you later. Bye."

She clicked off and rolled her eyes. A looker? Why on earth would her dad imply she might find Rayce attractive? On the other hand, her dad did have a tendency to tease whenever she'd dated. He thought his jokes were much funnier than they really were.

Well. Rayce Ryan *was* all kinds of sexy.

She opened the back door used by employees and, starting toward the main areas, picked up her rounds that had been interrupted by the missing ornament debacle: ensuring all decorations were perfect.

It had been ten years since Cassandra had seen Rayce in person. Sure, she'd seen him on the news. The bar in the resort always had at least one of the TVs streaming the sports networks and especially focused on winter sports. Over the past decade, Rayce's face had been everywhere. The golden boy. The skiing wunderkind. The Olympic gold hopeful.

The man who fell.

On Rayce's first trip down the giant slalom at the Olympics last year, something had distracted him and he'd crashed. Hard. The viewing public had watched as he'd been carted off on a stretcher, only to surface a few days later to announce that his injuries had been devastating. He may ski again, but never professionally.

Cassandra recalled how her heart had dropped as she'd watched that interview. Tears had even rolled down her cheeks. To have trained and worked so hard for something and then to have it torn away in literal seconds. It had to have destroyed Rayce in ways she couldn't even imagine.

When her dad had suggested they hire Rayce as their seasonal ski professional, she'd thought it an interesting idea, but hadn't believed it would come to fruition. Was he even ski-ready? Did he want to continue in the sport? Even if only as an instructor? And really, would taking a teaching job fulfill him in the manner that Alpine ski racing had? It could only be a step down for the man who'd once reigned as a local sports hero, and she didn't have to wonder how occupying that lower step might affect his ego. *Cocky*, *charming* and *confident* were the keywords the media often used to label him.

As well, she hadn't said anything to her dad about Rayce having been The Boy She Could Never Have. All through high school she'd been entranced by him. Every girl with eyes and a gushy swooning heart had been captivated by his charming manner. He'd been a jock, a confident cute guy who knew all the girls wanted him and who had used that to his advantage. Rayce must have dated half her senior class at Whistler Secondary.

But he'd never given Cassandra a glance.

Until the Last Dance the night before graduation. When Rayce had walked across the gymnasium floor and asked her to dance, her friend Beth had literally shoved Cassandra forward. She'd been too stunned, utterly at a loss for words. The Boy She Could Never Have wanted to dance with *her*? Following the momentum of that shove, she had moved across the dance floor under the dazzling disco ball as if under a spell. Dancing with the dreamy guy! Hand in hand! Face-to-face!

Yet when he'd bowed his head to kiss her, warning bells had clanged. And she had made a run for it.

Cassandra regretted not accepting that kiss. Because she had always wondered: *what if?*

And she still did. Could they have been a thing? Might the kiss have led to dating and something more? At the time, she hadn't been aware of his plans to move. Rayce had left Whistler right after graduation to devote his life to skiing and travel the Alpine ski racing circuit, so it could have never become serious. But if she were honest with herself, over the years she'd never chased away the fantasies of *what could have been.*

Are you excited I'm here?

Yes, she was. But she'd had the presence of mind not to feed his ego.

Shaking her head and smirking, she shook away her silly thoughts and redirected her attention to the decoration hung on the wall just outside the lobby. There were twelve identical arrangements of blue spruce wreath and red velvet ribbon nestled with green paper presents throughout the resort. This one needed a little nudge to the left…

"Hey!"

Cassandra startled at the deep male voice that, after her initial surprise, settled into her skin as if a welcome burst of sunshine warming the crest of an icy summit.

"Sorry, didn't mean to startle you." Rayce looked over the arrangement, his summer sky eyes bright with enthusiasm. He twisted one of the tiny presents to the left, then nodded. "Perfect."

Cassandra adjusted the present back to the correct position it had been in. "Did you find the cabin to your liking?"

"Yes. I appreciate that I can live on-site for this gig. It's cozy. And the tiny fridge will store my protein drinks and veggies." He tapped the present, tilting it off-center.

Cassandra moved the present again, and this time held her hand over it. "You have access to our chef and the cafeteria. All included in your salary. Feel free to use it anytime it's open." She swatted at his hand as he moved toward the present again. "Don't touch!"

He mocked affront and then chuckled. A laugh capable of making her lose her train of thought. "Did you find the ornament?"

Ornament? Uh… Don't think about his laugh!

"Not yet." And now she had a deadline thanks to her dad. "I'm headed to the supply room now to go over it with a fine-tooth comb."

He hooked his thumbs in his jeans' front pockets. "I'll go along with you."

"What?"

"I'm offering my services, fair lady. The wind has picked up so I'm putting off my survey of the slopes until tomorrow. And lame excuses aside, I'm whipped from today's travel. Two airports with long layovers and screaming babies. I'm good at finding stuff. I once found a snowboarder buried under four feet of snow in the middle of a blizzard."

Cassandra swallowed. The image of a body buried under snow arrested all thoughts about making things perfect, replacing it with a hard press against her heart.

The Whistler ski resorts had their occasional accidents. With the Pacific Ocean so close the weather was unpredictable. Blizzards and avalanches were a part of the deal. She'd grown up with a healthy understanding of safe skiing conditions and when to give Mother Nature a wide berth.

"Cassandra?" He bent to search her gaze.

She didn't want to explain how his casual mention of finding the buried snowboarder affected her. And she had promised herself she'd move beyond the grief this holiday season. Which couldn't begin without that ornament.

"Sure." She nodded. An inhale drew in courage. "I'll accept your offer to help. Come along with me."

"Any day, all the time," he sang as she sailed down the hallway and turned to take a stairway to the lower level where the storage room was located. "So how's life been treating you since high school, Cassandra?"

Descending a few metal stairs, they landed in the basement, and she flicked on the lights. The main room was neatly ordered with storage labels placed high on the walls to designate different sections. Her mother's doing. Everything was neat as a pin.

"Life is fine, as always," she responded. Fine. But not marvelous. Yet.

With a regretful wince, she veered toward the interior decorations. All the plastic bins that had held the Christmas decorations were placed back on the shelves. Some had a few items sitting inside—probably broken ornaments—so she pulled one down and opened the cover. "You?"

"Well, you know, took a little spill recently. Turned my life upside down. Now I'm trying to get back into fighting form."

Nothing but a cracked red glass ornament inside this one. She replaced the plastic bin and pulled down another next to one Rayce tugged out. "Fighting form? Do you intend to train again? For more competition?"

He'd only signed on as the resort's guest instructor for the season. And her dad had thought that perfect. See how he worked out. Then they could decide whether to extend Rayce's contract. Cassandra had thought his injuries had been so serious he wasn't able to ski competitively again. The media had reported he'd gone through numerous surgeries to repair broken bones, torn muscles, followed with intense rehabilitation. Though she noticed no outward signs of damage, no limp or painful movement.

"I'm always training," he said. "Docs tell me I'll never be able to achieve the level I was at, but when someone tells me no…"

She caught his wink. It lifted a gasp at the back of her throat. And something warm did a little spin in her core. The man wielded a useful charm with that wink. And he was very aware of it, she felt sure.

"This job is my introduction back to the slopes. A way for me to test my body, see if it's willing and able to fight back to competition form. I have to give it a go. Prove to myself that it's possible."

"It's good to know you have recovered."

"Recovery is a state of mind. Or so my physical therapist tells me." He rapped the cover of the container. "What am I looking for?"

Reining in the rise of desire his wink had summoned, Cassandra focused on the task. "Star-shaped ornament made from tree branches. It has a photo of me and my mom in it."

With a nod, he checked the bin, then placed it back on the shelf. There were dozens of the containers, which they methodically worked through.

"So you're the manager of the resort," he said as he worked. "I always knew you'd accomplish something great."

"You did?" Which meant…he'd thought about her achieving that greatness? Interesting. "You never gave me a glance in school. I find it hard to believe you had taken a moment to consider my future."

He turned his back to lean against the plastic containers and crossed his ankles. A soft gray sweater stretched across his noticeably hard pecs and abs. Once she'd stared at his blue eyes in a magazine spread and decided to call his iris color *caught* because any woman who peered into his summery blues long enough would surely be so.

Rein it in, Cassandra!

"I thought about you a lot, Cassandra. Watched you, too."

"Seriously? Sounds a little creepy to me."

But really? He'd watched her? No. Impossible. It had been her who had slid the sly glances his way as they'd passed in the hallways, or who had always taken the route from math class to science by the gymnasium so she could peer through the glass doors and catch a glimpse of him spiking a volleyball or netting a basketball. He'd played all sports when not training for the slopes.

"Not like stalker watching you," he said. "But every time you passed me in the hall? I gave myself whiplash."

She laughed, then caught herself. How to handle such a revelation? Of course, it meant nothing now. If only she had known ten years ago that they'd been secretly exchanging glances. Might her fantasies have come to fruition?

"You don't believe me?" He reached for the highest bin, which was filled with ornaments, and set it down for her. He bent beside it and watched as she sorted through the damaged and faded pieces.

With his proximity, she inhaled. He smelled subtly of cedar, but more so of pine and an icy winter day. Which was about the best scent ever.

"You're hard to not notice, Cassandra. You were smart. Pretty. Still are. But your hair has changed, and I like it. Very snow princess."

She paused in her sorting. After high school she'd decided to brighten her natural blonde hair, and now she regularly went to the salon to touch up the few places where some strands of gold fought to be seen. She liked the platinum look. It suited her. Snow princess? She'd never thought of it like that, but she did have some repressed need to *let it go*.

Or at the very least, get on with life and stop allowing memories of her mom to bring her down. This Christmas would be filled with joy and happiness. If it killed her.

"What'd I say?" He tilted his head wonderingly.

The man's blue irises were edged with black. Stunningly sexy. Add to that his stubble and messily cropped hair that looked as if Christmas elves had run wild through it, and he was everything and more. There was a reason why all the sports magazines had featured him on their covers. Why major sports products had paid him millions in sponsorships. And one of the largest cologne manufacturers had tagged him to hock their product. Women melted when Rayce Ryan looked at them.

Cassandra was not immune to such melting. Every part of her felt warm and loose. *Caught*. If he were to lean closer...

"I think I've lost you." He thunked her forehead with a finger. "You in there, Snow Princess?"

The rude touch prompted her to lean away. "Don't do that. I was just thinking."

"Yeah? I know, you're thinking about that night we danced, aren't you?" His voice lowered to a husky baritone, which teased at her inhibitions. "I still think about that dance once in a while, too."

So did she. And yet. She was an independent, capable woman, and certainly not prone to romantic delusions. "Why? That was ten years ago. We were in high school. We've grown up now, Rayce. We've moved on. We've…"

So why was she making a big issue about him asking now? Did she still have a thing for Rayce Ryan?

Of course you do, and don't deny it!

And they were not delusions. Romance was… something she hadn't taken time for in years. And she felt the ache of that lacking connection and emotion as strongly as she grieved for her mother. Though certainly she didn't have the time or heart space for a romantic liaison right now.

"I wish I'd had the courage to ask you out," he said. "But you occupied an echelon I could never manage to reach no matter how high I jumped." He shrugged. "Guess it served me right that you wouldn't kiss me."

A delicate glass ornament clinked against another and Cassandra shoved the container aside, standing. She'd analyzed that unclaimed kiss in the days following the dance.

"I couldn't kiss you," she explained. "Did you expect I'd put on a show for the whole class? We were standing in the middle of the dance floor. Everyone was watching. I…" She stepped away from the bin and wandered toward the door.

And really? He'd left town but days later. She would have been left with a kiss and dashed hopes for something more. She'd made the right decision. At the time. She did not live in the past and would not respond to the regret that rose with memory.

Before leaving, she said, "I wanted my first kiss to be special. I didn't think it meant anything to you at the time." She made a show of checking her watch. "I need to be somewhere. Meeting. I'll catch you later."

She fled. Just as she had fled the dance floor ten years ago. And it felt as silly and heart-wrenching now as it had then. She didn't want to run away from Rayce. She wanted to lean in closer. Inhale his subtle cologne. Savor his body heat. Feel his muscles meld against her body.

Kiss him.

Like she'd dreamed of doing for years.

Her reason for running away from his kiss had been because she'd wanted it to be special? To not be a performance before their entire class?

Standing atop a sunlit slope on his second day at the resort, Rayce's smile beamed brighter than the sun. If he'd understood Cassandra correctly, she *would* have kissed him if the conditions had been right. Which meant she hadn't fled his kiss because she hadn't liked him or because he'd somehow offended her. She had simply required the right moment.

Who would have thought? Since that night of the dance, Rayce had carried her rejection in the back of his heart, and it had often peeked out when at a party and he'd wanted to approach a woman. Would she like him? Would she want to kiss him? Or would she run away, leaving him standing there, the laughingstock of all those around?

Despite those anxieties, he had dated a handful of women over the years. But none of those entanglements had ever been so serious that his heart had relaxed enough to allow in contentment. Those women had been friends, lovers. A few weeks of excitement and fun between training camp and traveling from country to country. But dating seriously while he'd been on the racing circuit? Not easy. Except for that one time that had resulted in the ultimate betrayal.

Never date a team member, his coach had often advised. But had Rayce listened to that stern warning?

"Stupid heart," he muttered.

Now he was encouraged to learn that the rejection hadn't been because Cassandra hadn't liked him. Could he possibly find that moment with her once again? The perfect moment that would allow her to kiss him without an audience or the feeling of putting on a show.

He liked to make goals and exceed them. But this felt like more than a goal. It was…a quest! For a snow princess?

"Yes!" With a deciding nod, he pushed off down the slope.

His skis glided through the fresh powder. His plan this morning was to take things in, assess the runs he hadn't skied for years. There were hundreds spread across two mountains and various ski resorts. He'd take it slow and steady and focus on those closest to the Cobalt Lake Resort. He wasn't going to admit it to a soul, but a healthy fear made him cautious. One wrong move and the scarred muscles in his back would scream with pain. Not to mention his wonky leg.

The finest doctors had put him back together after his crash, but medical miracles weren't always possible. And while the surgery on his hip had been successful, the pain associated with the surgical scarring could quickly go from barely there to excruciating, shooting up and down his spine. It made him too cautious, fearful even, and that was never a good thing when racing down the slopes.

Rayce Ryan was broken. Yet admitting that

to himself felt defeatist. Like giving up. Had the doctors been right? Would he never again achieve competition form? Was he really out of the game for good?

He knew those answers. But his heart was playing stubborn and didn't want to accept that his future may look exactly as it did right now. Playing the role of ski instructor at a swanky resort.

He'd not trained for more than half his life to teach others how to navigate the bunny hill, or even to give cocky young ski-racing wannabes tips on how to hold their balance and find the fall line. But here he was. Life had dropped the Cobalt Lake Resort in his lap.

Might he possibly put back together his broken pieces here? Teaching required he listen and give others suggestions and approval. Yet how to get that personal coaching for himself? Was there anyone left in this world to pat him on the back and offer him the reassurance and love he craved?

That he'd included love in his mad-making thoughts surprised him. Yet it was the truth. He'd been alone for the last year. Perhaps for much longer than that, when he considered that racing, while surrounded by millions of spectators, was an insular sport.

Rayce craved the emotional support he'd once

received from his grandparents. And no, he'd never felt close enough to any of the women he'd dated to call it love. Rayce wanted a mixture of the approval and adulation racing had served him but with an even bigger portion of quiet acceptance. Maybe even respect.

And most certainly love.

Might he find that with Cassandra? She seemed to keep herself at a distance from him. There had even been a few moments when he thought she'd gotten lost in her thoughts—ah, shoot. He recalled his conversation with Brad on the way here. He had lost his wife, Cassandra's mom, two years ago in an avalanche. He'd mentioned Cassandra was still finding it hard to move forward, that grief was playing a real number on her.

And stupid Rayce had gone and said something about finding a person stuck in the snow after an avalanche.

"Idiot," he admonished himself.

Jabbing a ski pole into the snow, he shook his head. He might have already spoiled things with Cassandra, but that would never dissuade him from trying again and again.

CHAPTER THREE

THE NEXT DAY, while Cassandra waited for Kathy, the receptionist, to print up a copy of an invoice from a recent delivery, she adjusted the display of tiny resin snowmen featured at the check-in point. Five snowmen were seated around a fake fire warming their mittened stick hands. She couldn't remember if her mom had picked it up or it had been a gift from one of the guests. They were always receiving tokens and gifts from people who returned to Whistler year after year to spend their holidays here at the little boutique resort tucked between two larger establishments.

The Cobalt Lake Resort was a ski-in, ski-out that catered to an elite and moneyed clientele. They hosted many celebrity guests. Their security detail was top-notch, and Cassandra prided herself on the fact that not a single paparazzo had managed to invade their walls for a sneaky shot. They didn't close their doors to such individuals, but they did make it difficult to snag a room when certain high-profile celebrities were booked.

Rayce was considered a celebrity and she and her dad had discussed whether the hire would be wise. Certainly his presence would attract more guests, but for what reason? Merely to snap a shot with the famous skier? No, they'd decided Rayce would add another layer of polish to the resort's excellent reputation with his skills and easy charm. Fingers crossed, they would not be disappointed.

"What's up, Snow Princess?"

Cassandra jumped and one of the snowmen toppled. Was it the man's life purpose to sneak up on her?

"Must you do that?" she asked.

"I think I must. I like to shake things up. And you need to be shaken," he said with a huge helping of sly charm.

Shaken or caught in that beautiful blue gaze, she wondered. Feeling her jaw fall slack, Cassandra quickly noticed her swooning reaction and straightened.

Kathy, who stood over the printer, glanced over her shoulder at them. Cassandra did not miss the receptionist's bemused smile.

Rayce turned a snowman to face away from the fire. Cassandra turned it back to sit in line with his fellow snowmen.

"There's always one in the crowd that goes against the grain." He turned the snowman again. "Gotta have those sorts. They make life fun."

She curtly turned the snowman back. "Life requires a certain amount of order and..."

She almost said *control*. The need for order and perfection was naturally embedded in her DNA. Her mother had passed that gene on to her. And she would never *not* want to be like her mother.

"Talk to you later, Kathy," she said and resumed her morning route.

"I took a tour of the slopes." Rayce followed her through the lobby. The next stop was the spa to ensure they'd received the laundered towels and check that all the decorations were in perfect order. "Place looks great. You guys updated Lift Number Three. It's smooth. And a hot chocolate bar at the bottom of the Surf's Up run? Genius."

"We have three hot chocolate bars and a s'mores bar near the fireplace out on the patio. They are always busy."

"Your man, Eduardo, mixed me up a spicy cinnamon hot chocolate." He kissed his fingertips and followed with an, "Ahh..."

"You'll never get back to racing form if you indulge in those decadent treats."

"Eh. I'll work it off."

Out the corner of her eye she noticed him

ease a palm down his thigh. The injured leg? She wanted to ask, but she also wanted to respect his privacy.

"I'm going to do a run-through of a private training session tomorrow," he said. "Work out my game plan before you unleash me on your guests."

"That sounds like a good idea."

"It does, right? But I need a guinea pig. Someone to role-play the guest. Can you spare anyone to fill the role of newbie for me?"

"I'm not sure. Tomorrow we're training some new serving staff. Most other positions will be running extended shifts as the holiday rushes in on us."

Rayce spun around in front of her and landed his palm against the spa door. His eyes slowly took her in from head to toe in a manner that touched every nerve ending she possessed. Tiny fires ignited at each point. For once Cassandra regretted that she always wore white. The warmth suffusing her skin—was she blushing?

"What about you?" he said with a waggle of his brow. A suggestive move. And not at all businesslike.

Must she draw a line about lusting after employees? The resort didn't have any fraternization rules. It seemed an unnecessary intrusion into a person's private life. But how to stop sexy thoughts of Rayce when his wink was engineered at a DNA level to make a woman blush?

"Me? Uh…" Surely there was an employee she could spare for a few hours?

"I know you're busy. You are always on the go," he added. "I was thinking of asking your dad. I probably should—"

"I'll do it." Her heart answered before her logical brain could stomp a foot down in protest. Because really? There was nothing whatsoever wrong with working with the man to ensure he had his game down right. The bonus would be that she'd have reassurance their instructor had been a worthy expense. "I can mark some free time into the afternoon."

"Awesome. Find me on the bunny hill tomorrow. You can play my newbie skier."

"I'll see you then."

"Not if I see you first." She caught his wink as he opened the spa door for her and gestured grandly that she enter. "On the slopes, Snow Princess. I can't wait."

The door closed behind her, and Cassandra stood there a moment in the steamy, humid atmosphere to register what had just happened. The man had seduced her into working with him. She wouldn't call it anything but. Trying to resist that sexy wink and his charming manner had been futile.

And yet. The practice session may be more than an employer assessing an employee. Especially if that wink were doing its job correctly. And yet…skiing. She hadn't been on skis since her mother's passing. And she wasn't sure she was ready for it yet. Would it seem rude if she canceled? No, she didn't want to cancel. And it wasn't as though it were a date. Just a friend helping a friend.

Oh, how she wanted to allow a man into her life. Thing was, she wasn't sure her heart was in the right place to handle romance when grief still managed to overwhelm her at the oddest of times.

Honestly? Cassandra Daniels was incapable of change.

On the other hand, spending more time with the exuberant and charming Rayce might inject a little joy into her life. And that was a necessity.

Cassandra lived in the family wing of the resort, whereas her dad lived in the family home in town. Occasionally she considered moving back into town, finding a nice cozy condo, but the job kept her busy and staying close to work was key.

Or that was the story she told herself. She was no busier than most resort managers really, and she could have managed time off and even a vacation if she'd wanted it. But without children of her own, or even a boyfriend, it had been easy enough to lose herself in the job. Owning a home equaled a settled heart to her. Only a dream.

Her top-floor apartment looked out over the tiny Cobalt Lake and consisted of a bedroom, a small kitchen, a living area with a balcony that she spent a lot of time on even in the winter months, thanks to the heater, and an office corner, where she now sat going over the day's to-do list. It was the morning of her practice lesson with Rayce. Concentrating on the list was difficult due to the nervous flutters in her stomach. Why had she agreed to a ski lesson? Of all things?

A quiet knock on the door was expected. And a welcome distraction from *other* distractions.

"Come in, Anita!"

The sous chef stopped in every morning at seven o'clock with a pot of thick creamy hot chocolate. Cassandra had never asked her to do so; it was simply a continuation of what Anita had done for her mother. After Cynthia's death, Anita had taken a few days off, then quietly returned to work. Cassandra still hadn't spoken to her about her mother's death. They knew they shared a mutual grief and that was enough.

"With a touch of peppermint today," Anita said as she set the tray beside Cassandra's elbow on her desk. They never chatted overmuch. In the mornings Anita was busy prepping the day's meals for hundreds of guests. She turned to leave, but at the door paused to say, "The surprise is not my fault."

With that, she quickly closed the door.

"Surprise?"

Cassandra twisted her mouth as she studied the tray. A white porcelain pot of hot chocolate and an upside-down cup. A serving of Chantilly cream always accompanied the drink, and a mint cake sat beside it on a small plate. That woman would fatten her up sooner rather than later with all her sugary offerings.

Turning the cup over Cassandra gave a start and almost dropped it but managed to catch the cool porcelain before it clinked against the plate. Sitting under the cup was a tiny resin snowman. The very snowman Rayce had wanted to turn against his fellow snowmen sitting around the fake fire.

"Seriously?"

Shaking her head, she plucked up the figurine. What did this mean? It had certainly come from Rayce. And the fact that he'd learned where, exactly, to place it, and who he needed to know to do so, must have taken some sleuthing.

Interesting. Did that mean he was pursuing her? Or just making fun?

Probably the latter. And yet he'd told her he'd noticed her in school. A lot.

Cassandra pressed the snowman against her heart. "I should have never run away from that kiss."

On the other hand she was a private person. Even as a teenager she'd had the sense to be cautious. Had she kissed Rayce Ryan on the dance floor in front of their classmates, surely the gossip would have blazed. And in those situations it never ended well for the girl. And then with him leaving a few days later?

She'd made the right choice. At the time. But might the opportunity for a kiss again present itself?

"I wouldn't run away if it did."

With a nod, she set the snowman on the tray. Pouring the hot chocolate, she then topped it with a plop of Chantilly cream. It was a recipe from a famous Parisian restaurant that the resort paid to use exclusively. It was literally the reason some guests stayed; for the rich soul-hugging hot chocolate.

With a sip of the thick sweet concoction, she closed her eyes and remembered the first time her mom had told her about the Paris she dreamed about visiting, and how someday they would visit together. They'd climb the stairs to the top of the Eiffel Tower, stroll through the city's many formal gardens and share a pot of hot chocolate, even if it was summer.

They'd never gotten a chance to go to Paris. Tickets had been purchased for a spring trip. The spring following that deadly winter two seasons ago.

With a sigh, Cassandra caught her chin in hand. She'd gifted those tickets to a friend and her new husband as a honeymoon trip because she hadn't been able to bear going alone or with anyone else. She was trying to honor her mother with the beautiful decorations this season, but every time she thought about Cynthia Daniels's bright smile and tendency to use the occasional French word because she thought it was chic her heart dropped.

"I miss you, Mom."

And no amount of decorations—no matter how perfect—would ever bring her back.

Her dad had fallen in love with Faith, his new fiancée, just a month ago. Brad Daniels was moving forward in life. And Faith had two children Cassandra's age. She was going to be a stepsister! And that felt exciting. Yet every so often, if she were honest with herself, she felt as though her dad were cheating on her mom.

Silly, really. Her mom and dad had been not so much a perfect couple as a perfect team. Yet Cassandra, being an astute twelve-year-old who learned a lot about relationships from social media—and who could add and figured out she had been conceived months *before* her parents' marriage—had asked her parents if they'd *had* to get married because of her. The explanation had been simple: on the same day as their engagement party they'd also found out they were pregnant. Best day ever! Since then Cassandra's life had been filled with love and happiness. Brad and Cynthia Daniels had shared twenty-eight years together. Happily.

Yet even knowing her mother for twenty-eight years, it had still been too short a time. How to move forward as her dad had? When Cassandra felt memories tugging at her, she tended to grow straighter, become more controlling. While her dad had tended to head out for a run to be by himself with his memories.

The stress of the past few years, of holding back her sadness, had begun to weigh on her. She'd exploded over a missing ornament. She should have never done that in front of the employees. And this silly little snowman didn't have to be facing a specific direction to look inviting and cute to the guests.

Always one that goes against the grain.

Like Rayce Ryan?

Yes, the man—an adrenaline junkie to the core—went against everything her heart agreed was safe. But why did she require safety? Why not enjoy a little fun with a guy who made her smile? It didn't have to become a relationship. She hadn't the room in her heart for that right now.

Cassandra sighed. "Not yet. But…"

Maybe sooner than she expected?

Rayce had joined Brad Daniels for an impromptu lunch. Meeting him as they'd turned to walk the same hallway, Daniels had invited him to try the new hot Cuban sandwich the chef had created. They currently stood in an alcove attached to the kitchen, which was stacked with cases of wine and a trolly loaded with fresh produce. The sandwich, spicy yet loaded with cool sweet slaw, had hit the spot.

"Ready to hit the slopes?" Brad asked.

"You bet. You've got some smooth runs. And the powder you're making on the Blackout run is nice and dry. Perfect conditions."

"How's it feel to get back out there?"

Rayce's back twinged but it wasn't from pain, rather expectation. He knew what Brad was implying. Are you capable? Am I paying for a wounded instructor who won't be able to give it 110 percent?

"I'm at ninety percent, Mr. Daniels. Honestly? I can't take the runs at top speed, and my balance sometimes goes out because…" The pain made him leery. No one was going to know that. And honestly? That 90 percent was closer to 80. "I've developed a workout routine. I'll be getting good use out of the weight room. I hope to live up to your expectations."

"Don't push too hard, Rayce. I don't have any expectations. Just give it what you've got and represent the resort with kindness and respect. The guests aren't expecting you to medal in their presence. Sharing your knowledge and demonstrating good skills is what they are looking for."

He fist-bumped Rayce, then nodded to the chef who had been lingering nearby for a few seconds.

"I have to give the chef my report on the sandwich. You good to go?"

"Thanks, I am. I've arranged a practice session later to work on my teaching skills."

"Sounds smart. I knew I hired the right man. Tell Cassandra I approve of the new menu item when you see her." He winked.

"I, uh, sure." How did he know Rayce was going to see her soon?

Before he could ask, Brad wandered into the kitchen and started chatting with the chef.

Rayce shrugged and made his way out the back of the kitchen and down a hallway that led him to an outer door. He stepped out into the crisp winter air. The sun was bright and after that conversation he felt weirdly bright himself.

The man didn't have expectations? Everyone had expectations of Rayce Ryan. He'd lived his entire life to achieve goals, meet expectations, then crush them all and soar beyond.

It felt unusual to hear someone say to just do what he could. Almost as if whatever effort he put in would be acceptable. And yet how to function without the approval of a job well done? A goal achieved? A time smashed by a tenth of a second?

This not-meeting-expectations was a new experience for Rayce. And navigating it was going to prove a challenge.

CHAPTER FOUR

IF A PICTURE were featured in the dictionary depicting *snow bunny*, then the vision walking toward Rayce would hold place on the page. Dressed in white snow pants and jacket, with a fuzzy pink hat topped by a big pink pom-pom, and spills of her snow-white hair falling out across her shoulders and back, Cassandra's pink lips drew his attention like a target. Each time he saw her, he felt like the high school jock who had zero chance with the smart girl all over again.

Of course Cassandra was hiding grief under that bright smile and carefree demeanor. During the interview, Brad had mentioned she hadn't hit the slopes since her mother had passed. That was crazy. But Rayce knew grief. It could level a person. He'd be cognizant of her feelings. But as well, he couldn't bear knowing she might never step into a pair of skis again. This could be good for both of them.

"I wasn't able to find an available employee,"

she said as she neared him, "so you're stuck with me."

She'd been trying to find a fill-in so she wouldn't have to work with him? Yikes.

"*Stuck* is the last word that comes to mind." He winced. Had he sounded too eager, too excited that he would get to spend time with her? Could she sense his growing warmth and the need to unzip his jacket—but he wouldn't do that, because what would he tell her? She was so beautiful. And she kept dashing her gaze from his like a gazelle dodging the hunter. Cute.

And yet she'd tried to find a replacement.

Chill, man. The woman isn't interested in you. Pay attention to your job.

"Feels like we're getting some snowfall soon," she commented. "Maybe it'll hold off until nightfall. I want the snow groomer to make a run over the slopes before then."

Rayce nodded in approval. "I do love a night storm. Especially when there's a full moon."

"Oh." Cassandra dropped her gaze and studied the snow. In fact he sensed from her body language she didn't want to be here right now. "Well, I don't think it'll be an all-out storm. Just some flakes."

Had he said something to upset her?

Keep it professional, idiot.

He did want to try out his instructing skills

on a stand-in before the real thing happened, so he'd do his best to keep her smiling. "Should get enough to make guests happy campers come sunrise, eh?"

"Huh? Oh. Yes." She shook her head as if jogging something from her thoughts. "So. Here I am."

Oh, yes, she was. The one woman who seemed capable of throwing him off-balance with a mere look. Or a pause in her thoughts.

He had to focus.

"Okay, class!" He clapped his hands together, which lifted her chin, and earned him a small smile. Whew! "I understand you've never skied before, is that right?"

"Right," Cassandra answered astutely.

"Well then, we're going to spend a little time learning the basic maneuvers, ways to move and how to coordinate hands with feet before we even put on skis. It's all in the hips!"

He gave his hips a sway and that got a laugh from her, which made the pain that shot up his spine bearable. Just get through this, he coached inwardly. Don't let her see you fall.

"I knew you had a smile in there somewhere, Snow Princess. Show me your hip action. Let's go side to side and then in circles."

For the next twenty minutes he worked through basic motions that would allow someone new to the sport to get connected with their body and understand how certain movements would affect their placement on the snow. He kept it simple; if he sensed a skier was experienced, he would adjust his instructions accordingly.

Standing behind and near Cassandra was the best position to teach. And the occasional touch to her elbow to correct her arm position, or even to her shoulder to lower her line of balance thrilled him more than it probably should. It wasn't like he was touching her skin. But their intimacy teased at him. Her shiny hair beckoned for a nuzzle. And she smelled like flowers blooming under a crisp winter snow.

Keep it cool, he reminded. *Save the flirting for later, yeah? The quest for a kiss must be achieved.*

"Do you think that's helpful or a waste of time?" he asked when she laughed at another of his exaggerated hip swings.

"Very helpful. I see so many people stiffen up and try to prevent falls. If they were only taught the basics of body proprioception, they might not struggle so much. And we'd have less sprained wrist and ankle reports. Good call on the basics."

"That means a lot, coming from you."

"Oh, please, you're the Olympic athlete." She gave him a gentle punch to the bicep and he responded with mock outrage. "You know what you're doing."

"Sure, but I've never taught before. And was I kind? I distinctly recall your dad using that word. Be kind to the guests."

"You are a mix of kind and sensual—er, I mean…" She twisted her mouth. "You're a natural, Rayce."

Sensual, eh? That had slipped out before she'd caught herself. *Interesting.* So maybe he was getting through to her in the manner he'd hoped for? Was it possible that her repeatedly asking him to readjust her stance with his hands to her hips had been not so much because she had no clue what to do, but rather because she'd wanted him to touch her?

"Good," he said around an inner grin of triumph. Wouldn't pay to get cocky while in practice mode.

Remain professional.

Was that even possible? "I hope my limp doesn't show too much. Wouldn't look good coming from someone who's supposed to be a master at the sport."

"I hadn't even noticed it!"

"Really?" Even if she had said that to be nice, it relieved a niggling self-conscious worry. "It only bugs me now and then."

"Will you tell me about the injuries you suffered? The press made it sound like you'd never walk again. Yet here you are, looking like you could do the giant slalom and the super G on the same day."

"On a good day? I might take that bet. On a not so good day, my entire left leg seizes up. I've got some pins and titanium rods here." He tapped his upper thigh. "And a plate that's still holding my femur together."

"Yikes. Can you feel all that hardware?"

"No, but I do get good Wi-Fi reception."

Her jaw dropped. Then she quirked a wondering brow.

"I'm teasing," he insisted. "But I had you fooled for a second there."

"Fair enough."

Man, she was gorgeous. And not like the ski bunnies he was used to hanging around and on him. There was something about Cassandra Daniels that set her apart from any woman he'd ever had eyes for. It went beyond her beauty. She was perceptive, listened and seemed genuinely interested in what he had to say. Yet she wouldn't agree with him for agreement's sake. The woman had a mind of her own and wasn't afraid to use it.

"Have you had physical therapy to help with the pain?" she asked. "What about medication?"

"Too much physical therapy. Spent a lot of time in a recovery unit. And then a rehabilitation house. I'm on my own now. Incorporating all that I've learned from physical therapy. I have some chronic pain from the hip surgery, which compromised my skeletal alignment. It's crazy. As for drugs, no way. I didn't want to take pain-killers too long. So don't worry, I'll pass the resort's drug tests."

"We don't do that. And we wouldn't dream to do so. It's good to hear you're managing the injury. Just don't push it too hard. You've already shown the world what you are capable of."

"But did I?" Rayce stabbed the ski pole, which he'd been using to demonstrate balance, into the snow. "I crashed on my first jump out of the start house, Cassandra. That's hardly showing the world my stuff. It's a hell of a lot of failure if you ask me."

"Oh, come on, Rayce. Is that all you use to measure your success? How many World Cup Championships do you have?"

Two. And the World Cups were the sport's standard of excellence. Rayce had garnered the best and highest paying sponsorships from his World Cup wins. And by investing wisely, he had saved more than enough to live comfortably.

"The Olympics isn't the be-all and end-all," Cassandra said.

"Actually, it kind of is. If you can't medal in the big O, then you're nothing according to the media. Especially after your sponsors have invested so much in you. Millions, Cassandra. They certainly didn't get their money's worth from me."

"I guess I know that the energy drink dropped you."

"And the sportswear line. And the ski-gear line. And the protein drink that was going to be modeled after my own recipe."

"Yikes. I didn't know about those others. That's gotta be…"

"A mean slap in the face."

She sighed and nodded. "But you're not a failure, Rayce. Failing is not getting back up and moving forward. Failing is lying there and accepting it."

Her words sounded good. In theory. But. "Failure is not winning."

"Winning is everything?"

He blew out a breath. "Yes."

Winning used to be everything. But was it still? Of course it was.

And yet he knew that ultimate win was now out of his grasp. Much as he wanted to fool himself with training and therapy, the pain reminded him every morning that he could never go back to what he once had. No more World Cups. No more Olympics. He. Was. Broken.

"Whatever." He gestured dismissively. "I'll never come to terms with it. And I'll always pursue the next approving pat on the back. There's nothing anyone can say to change that. So!" He clapped his gloved hands together. "How about we strap on the skis and try the bunny hill?"

"Sure, but…Rayce, this probably doesn't mean much…" She lifted her eyes to meet his and he swallowed awkwardly. A certain truth glinted in her blue irises. It felt real, and familiar. *Comfortable*. "Whether or not you believe it, you have accomplished so much more than the average person. You don't need to prove anything to me, or my dad. We hired you—"

"Because everyone wants to train with Rayce Ryan. Don't deny it. And I get it. I am taking the paycheck."

"It's not all like that."

"But some of it is, right?"

She shrugged. His mood had soured since the conversation had switched to a focus on his weaknesses. And he didn't like to show that side to anyone, especially not a woman he was interested in.

And yet her father had said much the same. That Rayce didn't need to prove himself to him. He still didn't know how to process that declaration. But he'd have to learn if he wanted to glide toward the future instead of laying sprawled on the snow in the past.

"Skis," he said and handed her a pair.

He clicked into his own skis and waited as

Cassandra set hers on the ground and took position with her boots placed on either side of them, ski poles in hand. She stared down at the skis for such a long time he wondered what she was thinking about. And then he knew. This was a test for her. Brad Daniels had said his daughter hadn't put on skis since her mother's death.

Due to an avalanche.

Was it too soon? Had his invitation been thoughtless?

"I can't do this." With a sudden jerk of the poles, she stabbed them into the ground and stepped away from the skis. "I'm sorry. I...just can't."

She turned and walked off, her pace quickening to a jog.

Every bone in Rayce's body wanted to rush after her, but he'd felt something in her tone. A deep sadness. Tinged with fear. He knew that tone and that feeling. Man, did he know fear. He'd lost a part of himself during that Olympics' crash. He knew she had suffered a huge loss as well. It wasn't simply the lost ornament that was keeping her pinned to her grief; it was the memories of her mother, too.

He should go after her, make sure everything was okay. But the sadness in her voice reminded him so much of his own pain. A pain that had been with him far longer than since the accident. There were days he could barely deal with it himself. How could he help anyone else when he couldn't help himself?

Turning and stabbing his poles into the snow, he debated taking a run on the bunny hill. His leg didn't bother him today. Navigating the beginner hill would be like talking in his sleep: a no-brainer.

But.

Something compelled him to swing a look in the direction Cassandra had fled. Gathering the skis and poles, he put them away in the equipment shed, then went in search of Cassandra.

CHAPTER FIVE

THIRTY MINUTES AFTER she had fled the practice session with Rayce, Cassandra heard a quiet knock on her apartment door.

She swore softly and tugged the thick chenille blanket tighter about her shoulders. As soon as she'd gotten to her apartment, she'd kicked off her boots, shed her winter wear and plunged onto the couch. The tears that had been but a trickle had exploded and she'd engaged in a good sob session.

Now she sniffed softly and lifted her head to stare out at the sun falling behind the mountain. Her entire life had revolved around those mountains and the ski-bunny lifestyle. It had given her the greatest joy.

And it had devastated her family.

"Cassandra, I'm coming in," Rayce announced as he opened the unlocked door. He spied her sitting before the balcony doors. "No, don't get up. Is it all right that I'm here?"

Was it? She hadn't expected him to let himself in but asking him to leave felt rude. "Sure."

She nuzzled her chin into the blanket. No time to worry if she had red eyes or looked a mess. The man of her dreams carefully approached in the dimly lit room. Less than an hour and it would be completely dark outside. Still, the pale light seemed to outline his rugged jaw and even glint in one eye, softening him.

"I was worried about you," he said. He glanced around the room.

Everything was neat and in order. As it should be. All was well. Except her heart. Her grieving heart.

"Is it okay if I sit with you?"

Yes. No! She wasn't sure what she wanted right now. She'd never been one to share her emotions with others. And the only times she had, had been with her mom when they'd chatted over a hot chocolate. The Daniels family was not emotionally demonstrative.

But with Rayce's expression bordering on worried, she couldn't allow him to suffer.

She patted the couch beside her. "I'm sorry, I had a weird moment out there. Had to get away. I didn't want you to see me break down. And yet…" She shrugged and splayed her palms up in defeat. "Here you go. Cassandra Daniels. Undone."

"I'm sorry. I, uh… Your dad mentioned your mom's death during the interview. He also said you hadn't been on skis since then. So when I asked you to help me, well, I thought maybe if I could get you back on skis…" He sighed. "It was too soon. I shouldn't have pushed you."

She flashed a look at him. That he was so perceptive of her emotions startled her. It wasn't merely the light that had softened him; perhaps he did understand her. And it wasn't too soon, it was simply difficult. That he'd nudged her in an attempt to help meant a lot.

"I'm sorry, Cassandra. Losing a parent can be rough. Enough of a reason to need to get away when life zaps you with memory. Is that what it was out on the bunny hill?"

She sighed heavily and tugged up the blanket around her neck like a protective piece of armor. "Mom and I were close. We shared clothes, spent weekends shopping and enjoying spa treatments. We were best friends. We were extremely type A and—fine, I admit it—controlling. But together we were a dream team. That's what dad always used to call us."

Rayce sat on the couch beside her, facing the balcony doors. Snow had begun to fall in thick goose down flakes. That she had allowed him in and shared something so personal with him startled her. She hoped he wouldn't overstep and delve too deeply into her pain. She didn't know how to open up completely.

Yet at the same time she was thankful he knew about her loss. His presence comforted her. She was glad he'd thought to check in on her.

"Your mom must have been beautiful," he said. "I mean, look at her daughter."

"She was gorgeous. Always dressed in gray and black. Very elegant, and looking like, well… if I'm the snow princess, she was the snow queen."

"I sit in the presence of royalty."

She chuffed. The man had lightened her mood by being himself. Letting down the blanket, she turned to face him, leaning her shoulder against the back of the couch.

"It was the skis," she confessed. "Standing there, looking down at them. The last time I skied was on a sunny afternoon with my mom."

He smoothed a hand over her knee. Patted it gently. But that he didn't try to offer condolences or empty sympathy meant so much. After the funeral many had come up to her and said *let me know if you need anything* or *call me if you need anything*. Really? Why couldn't they simply *do something* for her, without her having to put herself out there in her most vulnerable time and ask?

Rayce's silence shimmered as if gold. Like the

best gift anyone could have offered regarding her loss. And she relaxed, settling into the couch.

"I'm not sure I'll ever be able to bring myself to put on skis again," she said quietly. "I…I see bad things when I even think about it."

"Bad things?" Now his gaze didn't so much catch her as offer her a soft place to fall.

She gave a deep exhaled breath laden with sadness. "My mom loved to ski at midnight. Under the full moon."

"Aw, Cassandra, I'm sorry. And I made that thoughtless comment about—I shouldn't have said anything."

He had said something about nighttime snowstorms. Which had been a catalyst to her mood swiftly changing. Yet she'd tried to remain light, not show him her angst, and paying attention to his teaching had helped some. There had even been a few moments of subtle flirtation she hadn't ignored.

"One night Mom went out alone." She spoke the words before her brain could hold her back from the confession. "She triggered an avalanche. It was hours before Dad realized she was missing. This was before we started using the GPS badges. Rescue crews worked through the night. We couldn't find her until the following morning." She buried her face in the blanket.

Her heart seized and her throat felt too narrow to breathe as her sobs renewed. She had cried often in those weeks following her mom's death. And every week after. Though the tears had lessened, the loss still felt the same in her heart. There was a hole now. In the shape of Cynthia Daniels. And nothing could fill that empty shape. Not even a silly ornament. That was still missing. The clock was ticking toward the turning on of the tree lights. She'd searched all the storage bins again, and the linen storage room. Would she ever find it?

Rayce gently squeezed her shoulder. Dare she ask him to wrap his arms around her? To hold her? It's all she had ever desired during those long winter nights following the funeral—to be held. Of course she and her dad had hugged, but he had been mired in his own grief. And initially neither of them had known how to interact with the other.

"Thank you for telling me that," he said quietly.

She wiped the tears from her cheek and braced her palm against the side of her head. "I hadn't expected such a visceral reaction to standing over the skis and looking down at them. Guess I know now that skiing is not in my future."

"It makes me sad to hear you say that," he said. "Skiing is such a joy, a passion, a way of life."

"I know." The sport affected a person not

only physically, but also mentally. It provided health. Activity. Utter joy. To completely abandon it seemed unthinkable. Even Rayce, who had been damaged irreparably by the sport, had not given it up. "But I don't know how to be comfortable with it again."

"You don't have to put on the skis," he said. "Not yet."

She tilted her head, one eye revealed above the blanket. He brushed the hair from her lashes. That touch went a long way in broaching the soul-encompassing hug she desired. They were friends, but not yet close enough to ask so much from him. Just having him sit beside her calmed her worries.

"Someday you'll have to put them on," he said. "You can't run from it forever. Trust me. I know grief, Cassandra. It's a deep pain. But it softens over time. And I promise, when you're ready, I'll be there to hold your hand when you glide down the slope. I'm sure your mom would wish the same for you."

She'd never thought of it that way. Cynthia Daniels would never want to see her daughter in such emotional distress. So why had she done something so stupid as to go out on her own at midnight when she'd known the dangers and risks? Her selfishness had changed Cassandra's life forever.

"Is there anything I can get for you now?" he asked. "Some tea? A box of tissues?"

She smiled at his genuine concern. "I'm going to be okay."

"Good, because it hurts my heart to see you sad."

"I wouldn't want to be the cause of a man's wounded heart."

"I heal fast." He rubbed his thigh. "Some parts of me do, anyway. Hey, I was thinking about taking a walk around the lake once it's dark. Check out the lights. Do you want to join me?"

"I'm…"

"Not sure. I get it. I shouldn't intrude any longer. I know grief can be so personal." He stood and then picked up the blanket that had fallen to the floor with his movement. He tucked it on her lap. "I wanted to make sure you were okay."

Cassandra inhaled his delicious winter scent. It distracted her from her sadness. The man was handsome, talented *and* compassionate? There had to be something wrong with him—but what?

"I'll, uh…be at the path to the lake in an hour. If you want to join me, I'll see you then."

When he stood at the door she called, "The snowman under my teacup was evil!"

Rayce smiled a wicked yet sexy grin. "Yes, yes, it was. I did tell you I was here to shake things up."

"Mission accomplished."

"Don't give me any high scores yet. I'm just getting started. See you later, Snow Princess."

She was thankful for his quick exit. And while she should have asked for that hug, she felt the little she'd given him had been an opening into her soul. And that opening beamed out some light.

Spending time with Rayce made her less sad. And all he had done was listen to her. But he had said he knew about grief. Perhaps they were kindred spirits who could help one another?

She dared to think that could be possible.

CHAPTER SIX

AN HOUR LATER Cassandra bundled up for a walk in the chilly weather and headed outside. A sudden *meow* distracted her, and she caught a glimpse of that darn cat. The stray that had been scampering around the Cobalt Lake Resort grounds since summer. Snow-white, it was difficult to see against the snowy landscape and tended to surprise her. It was becoming a nuisance, stalking the birds who conglomerated at the various feeders and leaving tracks across the guests' snow angels. And she was pretty sure she'd found cat hairs on the cushions around the outdoor fireplace. But she had a resort to run so there was no time to consider pet patrol.

Wandering across the patio where the fireplace blazed and a few guests sipped hot chocolates before the amber flames, she felt drawn toward the interesting safety Rayce offered. When she arrived at the head of the wood-paved pathway that circled the small lake and sighted the handsome athlete, she could only smirk. He was doing it again!

"Seriously?" she announced as she approached Rayce.

The man adjusted the big red weatherproof bow attached to the wood railing. Dozens of the bows were posted along the pathway. Christmas lights were strung between them. The glow from the lights reflected off the glass ice pond in fairytale glimmers. Cassandra would never tire of the photos guests posted on social media along with comments that the lake walk was *magical* and *enchanting*. One couple had even gotten engaged on the covered dock at the halfway point around the lake.

"Now it's right," he said with a pat to the now-crooked bow.

Cassandra tilted the bow to the right. Perfect. Then, feeling the best way to win the argument was by distracting him, she started walking. "You like to disturb the norm!" she called back.

He joined her, their winter jackets brushing softly as their arms touched. "I like to push boundaries."

"I'm aware of that."

"Why is it you are so satisfied with normal?"

An interesting question. She did like to be challenged. Yet there was a certain safety in familiarity. "What's wrong with normal? You make it sound dirty. Taboo."

"Nope, you've got that wrong. All the taboo things I can think of are far from normal. And some involve whipped cream."

Cassandra's jaw dropped open as she met his grinning face. With a waggle of his eyebrows, she realized he'd done it again. He was tossing out zingers to see if he could get a rise out of her. Disturbing her norm. Inciting a tremor of desire.

"I love whipped cream," she volleyed, taking a bit of pride in the quick reply.

"Then you and I are going to get along just fine."

They reduced their walking pace to a stroll as the path curved and overhead the tree branches danced with colorful lights. Pinks, blues, greens and reds reflected in the snow, dusting the branches and shimmering across the glassy lake surface.

"This is incredible," he said. "It feels like a fancy light show yet cozy at the same time. And Christmas music?" A melody softly echoed through the speakers placed along the trail. "Love it!"

She pointed toward the center of the lake. "As soon as we get safe ice thickness, we'll open it for ice skating and pond hockey."

"Nice. I love an aggressive game of pond hockey."

"Yeah? We'll see how talented you are with the stick when we meet on the ice."

Rayce nodded in surprised approval. "I think you just challenged me, Miss Not So Normal."

"I suppose I did."

"So I take it you're not a puck bunny?"

"Please." Puck bunnies were over-styled fashion victims who fawned over professional hockey players and flirted their way into their beds and sometimes earned an expensive and sparkly gift. "I'd never be caught swooning over the players from the sidelines. I like to get into the action."

"I never would have guessed that of Miss Astute and Perfect."

"Don't call me that. And I'm not Miss Not So Normal, either."

"Sorry. But can I use Snow Princess? Pretty please?"

She made a show of thinking it over, then nodded. "If you must."

"Yes!" Rayce glanced over his shoulder. "But that ribbon…"

"Fine!" She skipped ahead and turned to face him as they walked. "I admit that I have perfectionist tendencies."

His swagger drew attention to his hips. Relaxed, easy. So sure of himself. "You like to control the world."

She performed an evil laugh and then pressed

her pinkie finger to her lips. "Or perhaps just a small portion of British Columbia."

He laughed and jogged up to her, clasping her hand. "I love an evil plan. Now here's mine. Race you to the dock?"

"Doesn't sound very evil, but..." Dropping his hand, Cassandra took off. "I'm in!"

After a burst of energetic running, she arrived at the covered dock that had been built to showcase its Nordic design; it was made of clean pine, with traditional rosemaling along the rafters. Another couple leaving hand in hand nodded to her and she called to them to have a good night. That left the dock to Cassandra and Rayce.

Stepping up onto the cozy retreat beneath the glowing lights always lifted her mood. Spending time with Rayce seemed to do the same. Was it his teasing at her boundaries that felt so exhilarating? How odd. And yet she did enjoy inching closer to his idea of shaking things up. And she hadn't given a moment's thought to—no, she'd cried enough earlier. Time to take a vacation from work and her grief, if only for the evening.

With a leap over the two steps, Rayce landed on the dock floor with arms splayed triumphantly. "He makes it in a single bound!"

"I'm very impressed. I noticed your limp earlier and I thought you were in pain. Everything all right now?"

"Eh, there's some muscle twinges, but I'm still standing. And performing that stupid leap may seem silly but considering I couldn't even walk a year ago? I'm taking it as a win."

"You can have it."

"Thanks. That'll go a long way when I know I'll be suffering in the morning."

"Oh, Rayce, then why do you do such things?"

"How can I not? I'm stuck with an injured leg and tweaky back while all I want to do is push my body to the limits. If I keep pushing maybe my leg will take the hint and get over this stupid pain."

"Either that, or you'll cause more damage. Sorry. I shouldn't be a naysayer. What do your doctors say?"

"That I need to take it easy."

"Even the sports doctors? The ones who work with the Olympic team?"

He shrugged. "I lost access to them a month after being in the hospital."

"Really? That hardly seems fair."

"I don't want to talk about the politics of it all. I've survived and that's what matters."

"Fair enough." She tapped one of the hanging icicle lights. "So what do you think?"

"This place is cool." He looked out over the pond. Red and green lights dazzled the circumference, and a fancy laser light painted a show of

Santa's sleigh being pulled by reindeer across the iced surface. "Promise you'll include *The Little Drummer Boy* on the playlist for me?"

"Oh?" She assessed him. His eyes sparkled in the glow of the white icicle lights. And that hair…always tousled and so tempting. She'd like to run her fingers through it. Tug him closer and— "Is that your favorite Christmas song?"

"It is. I like the story of the little boy playing his simple drum for the newborn Christ. It…" He shrugged. "Gets me right here every time." He thumped his chest. "But don't tell anyone Rayce Ryan has a soft spot."

She crossed a finger over her heart. "Promise."

"I suspect you are an excellent secret keeper."

"The best. But if that's the only secret you've got…?"

"Eh, I have plenty. The press exposed most, though. Crazy how the paparazzi became so interested in a regular guy from a small town, isn't it? And yet I make one monumental mistake, and they've ghosted me."

Cassandra hadn't realized it but, yes, about a month after the Olympics snafu, all news of Rayce Ryan had fallen off the radar. What fickle allies the press could be. And the public, for that matter.

"Does that bother you? Not getting the attention anymore?"

He leaned against the railing, cocking his head to the side. Their breaths condensed before them in tiny puffs. "I am a guy who likes to put himself out there, be seen, make connections, talk to anyone willing to talk to me. The media fed that need. It's the part where my coach ghosted me that really cuts."

"Your coach? Seriously? You mean you haven't talked to him since…?"

"Not since about a week after the accident. He stopped into the hospital. Tossed a wilted bunch of flowers at the end of my bed and proceeded to tell me how disappointed in me he was."

"Oh, Rayce, I'm so sorry."

"Eh." He shrugged. "I deserved it. The man invested a lot of time and money in my training. And look what he got."

"He got a double World Cup champion is what he got. Not to mention you were rated number seven overall in Alpine racers. That's an accomplishment."

He sighed and scruffed his fingers through the hair she wanted to feel against her skin. "I know, but that didn't seem to matter much in that moment when he stood in the doorway to my hospital room. Coach had been there for me since I was a teen. He wasn't exactly a replacement for my grandfather, but he was protective and stood up for me and had my back. Until I crashed. He blamed me for making a stupid mistake. And he was right on the mark."

"Rayce! How could he have possibly blamed you for that? It was an accident."

His heavy sigh spoke volumes. "My mind wasn't in the game. I forgot that my goal was to please others. And now? Who will approve? Cheer me on?"

"You need the cheers but without the flashes," she stated.

"Maybe? But I'm not here to talk about my screwups," he said. "I thought we were talking about our social skills?" He slapped his chest. "Super extroverted. Complete opposite of you."

Cassandra conceded to his sudden need to change the subject. Though she wanted to know more, to delve deep into his soul and—really? She wanted to go soul-deep with the man? What had happened to just friends?

That charming smile and easy demeanor is what happened. Rayce defined irresistible. And that made her want to learn as much about him as she could. And might that abandoned kiss be claimed?

"I'm not an utter introvert," she said. "I can turn on the smile for our guests and clients."

"But I suspect you're happier when you get

some downtime. You go all day, make the world perfect, and then…?"

That he pinned her so easily made her wonder if it was as obvious to everyone else. Of course she'd observed as much about her mom. When Cynthia Daniels turned in for the evening, she shut down. Soak in a hot tub, sip some tea and forward all work emails to the *save* file. That had also been her time to spend with family. And while her mother had worked sixty-hour weeks, she had still found time for Cassandra, and made that time special.

But Cassandra had no one to give her attention to so pushing her workweek to seventy hours had been a natural progression. A social life? What even was that?

"After the world has been perfected," she said to Rayce's question, "I shelter in my room and have a cup of tea or hot cocoa and relax."

"Ah, so you are capable of relaxing."

"Oh, come on! I'm relaxed right now." She waggled her shoulders, letting her hands flop. The tension that usually strafed the back of her neck was, surprisingly, absent. "See?"

"Well, and there are no people watching right now." He made a show of casting his glance around them in a one-eighty.

Cassandra glanced around the pathway that circled the pond. The night glistened like a fairyland. The atmosphere around them encouraged her to be present, completely. To accept what life wanted to give her. "No, there aren't. But what—?"

"I did bring this." From his jacket pocket Rayce tugged out a plastic piece of greenery with white berries—mistletoe.

"Where did you get that?" She made a grab for it, but he easily dodged her. "You broke it off from some display—"

She swallowed back her protest as he held it high. Above and between the two of them. The unspoken question was so loud: *do you dare?*

"Don't run away this time." His voice was laced with a quiet request to meet his heart halfway. A heart that had been battered, beaten and put through the ringer.

In his eyes shimmered a softness. Gone was the cocky, confident skier who had once held the world's attention and who had thrilled the crowds with his swift and agile performances. The part of him that called out to her now felt almost innocent. Lost.

Similar to how she felt when grief overwhelmed her.

Stepping up to him, she eyed the piece of green plastic that dangled a few white berries. Suddenly they stood in the center of the high school gymnasium, disco lights flashing across their faces. Hands sweating. Heartbeats thundering.

But this time, they stood alone. No audience to dissuade her hopeful fantasy.

Cassandra tilted onto her tiptoes and—a snarling *meow* parted them both. Rayce spat out something about "a critter" and dodged to the left.

Cassandra now saw the white cat had gotten tangled in the Christmas lights strung along the pathway. It struggled manically. Crouching, Rayce approached the creature carefully.

From down the path some kids shouted to, "Catch the snow monster!"

With a quick move, Rayce succeeded in untangling the cat and it leaped from his hands, landing on the glassy lake surface. The cat struggled to find its footing on the slippery ice.

Two teenagers jumped onto the dock and raced to the railing to watch as the cat scrambled away.

"You guys weren't chasing that cat, were you?" Rayce asked in a surprisingly parental tone that impressed Cassandra with the added innuendo of admonishment. "Leave it alone."

"We won't hurt it, mister," one of the kids responded. "We just want to see if it makes it across the lake. It slipped! Did you see that?" He poked his friend in the arm.

The look Rayce gave her said exactly what

Cassandra was thinking: once again their kiss had been foiled. And it was obvious their window to try for another kiss would not return out here.

He held out his hand and she took it. They started toward the resort at a slow stroll. Little was spoken. The tension was palpable. The desire heating her neck had not lessened. She had been so close to finally kissing the one man who could knock her out of her self-imposed boundaries.

That darn cat!

When they neared the patio with the blazing fire, Rayce tugged her to a stop and she turned to look up at him. His skin and eyes glowed from the reflected Christmas lights.

"I'm not sure I'll be able to walk within your vicinity without wanting to kiss you," he said.

Same. And yet logical Cassandra leaped out to take control over mushy romantic Cassandra. "That wouldn't be wise in front of the employees."

His smile dropped. "You worried about some kind of fraternization thing? Because if you are, I'll quit the job right now."

"You haven't even begun!"

"I know, but that's the choice I'd make. Just so you know."

"It's not that. We're not so fussy about telling

our employees who they can date. I'm a private person. I like to keep things like…" *their almost kiss!* "…that…sacred."

He stroked her cheek. "I get it. You're not into cameras flashing while I sweep you off your feet and into a kiss?"

The thought horrified her. To see her mug splashed on some front page, or worse, go viral online? No, no and most definitely, no. She shook her head.

"Well, the paparazzi are no longer interested, so no worries there." He twirled the plastic mistletoe. "But I may attempt the sweeping part again when you least expect it."

She snatched the mistletoe from him. "I would expect nothing less from the man sent to shake up my life. Now, from where did you steal this?"

He grabbed it back and stuck it in the back pocket of his jeans. "Not telling."

"But if there's a hole in a display somewhere…"

"That'll keep you on your toes!" He took off walking on the path.

"Rayce!"

"Merry Christmas, ya filthy animal!" he called back, then sped up, his chuckles echoing in the chill night air.

Cassandra shook her head. But then she smiled. Quoting one of her favorite childhood Christmas movies? The man was certainly all kinds of crazy mixed with charm and a dose of dashing.

And he had almost kissed her.

Let the shaking up of her life begin.

CHAPTER SEVEN

ANITA SET THE serving tray on Cassandra's desk and left with a few kind words to have a great day. Finishing off a letter to the local scout troop who had requested a field day at the resort, Cassandra then turned over the cup and gave a little chirp to see a little drummer boy figurine smiling up at her.

She chuckled. "Oh, he's good."

She tapped the drummer boy's head. "You are almost as cute as he is. But he is handsome. And sexy. And..."

She sighed. Oh, that almost kiss. Closing her eyes returned her to the dock, standing so close to Rayce. His outdoorsy scent had filled her senses. The soft melody of Christmas music played in the background. One more inch and their breaths would have mingled, their lips would have touched.

Her heartbeats thudded now. She sighed and caught her cheek against a palm, eyes still closed.

What was happening between them? Were

they flirting toward something greater? The thought did not put her off. And it encouraged another smile. What a perfect way to spend the holiday season. With a man who intrigued, excited and surprised her. Cozy snuggles while sharing a blanket before the fire? Yes, please!

Of course she wouldn't expect anything more than a fun time. He had, after all, only signed on for the season. And certainly she wasn't prepared to begin a relationship, what with—well. She hadn't the time for that.

And yet, why *not* indulge while he was here? She'd seen the happiness return to her dad's eyes after he'd fallen in love again. It was a special spark that only lighted when a person's heart sang. And there was no reason she shouldn't seek a relationship. Her workload wasn't so immense she couldn't devote time to another person.

What was stopping her?

She glanced to her daily list. The top item was *find ornament*. How many days had she left on her dad's ultimatum to find it? Half a week had already passed.

Was searching for the ornament a means to fill the hole in her heart? Could she fill that hole and make room for another living, breathing person? Why couldn't she be satisfied with memories of her mom, and just forget about the wood star?

There were many more ornaments on the tree that her family had gathered over the years. Each with a different memory. Why not stroll out to the lobby right now and flick on the Christmas tree lights? Begin the holiday proper?

Something held Cassandra back. Pushed her toward the quest. And it was a different place in her heart that needed filling than that which was currently being entertained by Rayce Ryan.

It was the feeling.

Christmas isn't a season; it's a feeling.

Cynthia Daniels would often quote her favorite movie as Cassandra would follow her about the resort, helping to tidy.

That ornament had brought joy to Cynthia Daniels's heart. And by placing it on the tree this year, Cassandra would honor her mother's memory and move forward.

Only then could she exhale and allow another person into her heart space. *And feel.* For now she would steer clear of anything serious with Rayce Ryan.

They were eighty years old, the pair of them, and had been married for sixty years. Neither had skied a day in their lives. But it was on their bucket list, along with sky diving. That adventure was going to happen next week after they hopped on a flight south to Arizona.

Rayce got a kick out of watching Mr. and Mrs. Thorson glide down the bunny hill. Hands clasped to support one another, their elated hoots echoed in the crisp morning air as their extremely slow journey seemed to stir up more joy than any person should contain.

He shouted an encouraging, "Whoo!" and kept a careful eye on the twosome. They'd be fine. They wore enough winter clothing that should either topple, they'd probably roll in the thick snow like giant marshmallows.

With their general lack of ability and hearing, Rayce had taken his time with them, making sure they understood the movements and correct balance before allowing them to step onto their skis. He'd felt a flush of pride when they'd taken their first sweep down the hill. And not fake or false pride like an approving word that must be earned through hard work, pain and repetitive motions.

Now that he thought about it, Rayce wasn't sure he'd ever taken pride in his accomplishments. All his life he had known nothing but skiing. He'd read about it, talked about it, eaten on the slopes and dreamed about the powder through the night. His grandparents had pushed him down a hill when he was four and since that auspicious first descent, he hadn't stopped seeking the next thrill. What else existed beyond skiing? It wasn't as though he were qualified for a desk job or retail work. He didn't know how to exist away from the slopes.

The thought was crazy. And he knew it. But that didn't loosen the fear in his bones. Who was Rayce Ryan without the skis?

"Heck if I know," he muttered.

He winced as a step to the side tweaked the muscles in his back. That was the real fear that had become embedded in his bones. The pain made him tentative on the snow, even disconnected from his body at times. It challenged his balance. And ski racing was all about balance.

Was he a has-been? A loser? He didn't want to wear those labels. But the only way beyond them was by rising and taking back the win. Through immense and uncompromising pain. A win that he wouldn't know how to appreciate. So would it even be worth it?

A triumphant shout from the bottom of the hill redirected his thoughts.

Pushing off and taking the hill in a quarter of the time it had taken the Thorsons, Rayce arrived beside them as they both settled on a bench to rest after their strenuous but successful journey.

"You two rock," he announced. Mr. Thorson met him with a fist bump. Rayce hoped to remain as young at heart when he reached their age. "See you tomorrow same time?"

"For sure!"

"Glad you had a good time. Go have some hot chocolate!"

Helping them out of their skis, he then sent them off in the direction of the hot chocolate and s'mores bar. He collected their skis and poles and skied over to the rack to leave them for the groundskeeper who made a sweep every so often to return equipment to the warming room.

Thinking about hot chocolate reminded him of the clever message he'd sent Cassandra this morning. Hey, it was the little things, right? Deviously, he knew she'd spend time trying to figure out exactly where that figurine had come from.

At the sight of Rayce's cocky smile, Cassandra straightened from inspecting the massive wreath hung on a wall in the lobby. It was filled with tiny festive figurines. Yet nothing seemed to be out of place.

"Not from that one," he said as he joined her side. He beamed. So proud of his intrigue. "But I've got some mistletoe in my pocket if you want to learn where that came from."

"You think you're so clever?"

He shrugged. "I do have certain talents."

Cassandra exhaled. Yes, he did. And the idea of utilizing said mistletoe flourished in her brain to a full-on make-out fantasy. No stray cats struggling in a tangle of lights to stop it, either. But with a glance to the reception desk, she quickly swept away that titillating thought.

Kathy set down her headset and with a wave got Cassandra's attention.

"What is it, Kathy?"

"I got a call from Lift Four. The Torgerson twins are at it again. I tried to contact your dad but he's in a meeting right now."

"The Torgerson twins?" Rayce tilted a questioning glance toward her.

"They are young, rich, spoiled and tend to hit the slopes drunk. Anyone hurt?" she asked Kathy.

"No, but the attendant at the bottom of the lift said they've planted themselves on a snowbank and are loudly booing the skiers' landings."

"They need to be redirected," Cassandra said. "I'll round up one of the grounds men to help me coax the twins toward the nightclub. It's a bit early for dancing, but I'm sure they'll appreciate the atmosphere in there."

"I'll help you."

She gaped at Rayce, but then realized he may be just the person to help her out. The twins were celebrity chasers, and she was quite sure they lived only to see and be seen with everyone who was anyone.

"You may be the bait we need to lure them away from the lift," she said. "Come on."

Half an hour later Cassandra and Rayce said goodbye to the twins and headed outside to walk the path toward the lake. A guest had reported seeing animal tracks on the path. Possibly a bear? Cassandra doubted that, but she'd give it a look.

As soon as the twins had seen Rayce, they'd asked for autographs. Rayce had signed the sleeve of the one's ski jacket. After some polite conversation, and Rayce hinting that all the ski bunnies were in the bar warming up by the fireplace, they'd convinced them to take their hijinks inside.

Cassandra exhaled for a job well done. With a lot of help from their resident celebrity. But watching Rayce chat about his World Cup wins and his secret maneuvers hadn't felt like witnessing an ego show. In fact, the ego that had always puffed up his chest and set back his shoulders during after-race interviews hadn't been evident. And she wasn't sure if that saddened her or if it was just Rayce taking a new turn. Had the accident crushed his ego?

Before thinking, she blurted out, "What did it do to you?"

Rayce slashed a gloved hand across a pine

tree, releasing a storm of snow across his face. He turned and tilted his head. "What are you asking? About the twins? They're all right guys. Just needed some attention."

"I mean the crash." She shrugged. "You were so kind to the twins. I would have expected grandstanding and boasting from Rayce Ryan, especially with two devoted fans of the sport."

"Boasting? You think I'm cocky?"

"Rayce. The whole world knows that."

He bowed his head but couldn't hide his smile. "Fair enough."

"Yes, but since you've been here at the resort I've noticed, well…you seem calmer. Maybe not so quick to grab the spotlight?"

He clapped his hands together and studied the wood pathway. No animal tracks yet. She'd made him uncomfortable. But it was too late to take the question back. And she genuinely felt he was a different person than the one who'd skied competitively a year ago.

"I told you about my mom," she said. "It changed me and the way I interacted with others."

"Really? Because you seem like the same go-getter I once used to notice in high school. Still on the fast track, everything perfect, woe to all those who don't meet your standards."

That was a shocking statement. But before

Cassandra could reply that he was being hurtful, he put up a hand. "Sorry. That was, well, it was the truth. But that doesn't mean I haven't noticed your kindness toward the employees and your general goodness. You are a snow princess, like it or not."

"Does it come with a crown?"

He caught her teasing tone and winked. "Made of snowflakes. But you're right about me not grabbing the spotlight. Well. There are no spotlights to be found here at the resort."

"We keep a tight rein on the media."

"Appreciated. By all your guests." He scruffed his fingers through his hair, an action that always made Cassandra's fingers itch to do the same to him. Then he said, "You're right. This past year has changed me. Is it for the better? Not sure. What do you think?"

"I think you're…" sexy, alluring, and oh, did she want to kiss him "…doing well with the guests. And the staff. You've won them all over. Especially Anita. You and Anita have a weird thing going on."

"We do have a secret alliance. Does it bother you?"

She thought about the surprises that appeared under her morning cup. "I'm not going to tell you who you can befriend and who you can form secret alliances with. Anita was good friends with my mom."

"I picked up on that from the chats I've had with her. She's very proud of you. Following in your mom's footsteps. You know, that's the only thing I've ever wanted to feel about myself."

"What? Pride? You don't feel pride in your accomplishments? Rayce!"

"If I don't have a coach yelling at me to do better, change an angle, do it again and again and again, I just..." He shrugged and his shoulders dropped. "Maybe I won't ever get back to racing form again. And maybe I don't want to."

That was a stunning confession. What else was there for an Alpine ski racer like Rayce Ryan? Guest ski professional at a local resort didn't seem to land even close to what he was accustomed to.

"Really? What do you want?"

"I can't tell you. It's..."

At that moment, a rustle came from beneath the pine tree, which spat out a snarling white cat. It leaped out and dashed between them on the path and scampered off.

"That darn cat. Again!" Cassandra declared as she studied the ground. "Those are the smallest bear tracks I've ever seen." And what terrible timing the critter had. Would she ever find a moment alone with Rayce to fulfill her fantasy of kissing him?

"You should catch it."

"Oh, no. The last thing I need is a pet cat. It's feral, I'm sure."

"Yeah, but what if it wanders onto one of the slopes? When there are skiers out there? I'm sure you have accident insurance, but I'm also sure you want to avoid any lawsuits."

"I hadn't thought about that. But what would I do with the cat if I did catch it?"

He shrugged. "Take it to the pound. They can rehome it. It could be someone's pet. Maybe they are looking for it."

He had a point. "I'll get one of the employees on the task. Uh…" He had been about to tell her why he didn't think he wanted to race again. She wanted to hear that. But she was starting to feel the chill. If a body didn't move in the winter air, it felt the cold much faster. "Are you hungry?"

"Always."

"Would you like to join me for dinner as thanks for the suggestion about the cat?"

"I'd like to join you because you want to spend time with me."

"Oh. I do want to spend time with you," she said breathily. "Meet me at my room in half an hour. I'll have a meal brought up."

"It's a date." He wandered off toward the employee cabins.

Cassandra muttered what he'd said. "It's a date. Is it? Maybe. I suppose. Yes." She settled into the idea of it with a swoony smile. "Yes, it is."

CHAPTER EIGHT

THE YARD LIGHT positioned above the big outdoor fireplace highlighted the thick fluffy flakes in their magical freefall. They'd eaten a fantastic meal and shared a large slice of Triple Threat chocolate cake, dense and layered with cream cheese frosting and crumbles of chocolate bits and cherries. Cassandra only ate a few bites. When she'd pushed the plate across the table, Rayce had eagerly finished it off.

Now what better way to enjoy the snowfall than with a bottle of wine, while wrapped in a cozy blanket. The chilled fruity red hit her just right and she smiled as she relaxed deeper into the pillows propped behind her back and shoulders. This couch was deep and comfy, and placed before the windows for the perfect view of the mountains.

Rayce had commandeered a red-plaid blanket and sat close enough that she could breathe in his crisp winter scent and wonder how long it might be before they kissed. They were safe from any feline interruptions here.

"Favorite Christmas movie?" Rayce asked.

They'd been sharing their favorites while watching the snow flutter in the golden beam of light. Favorite sports, adventure spot, music, food, color, all the standards. It was a nice way to get to know him better. And that he had a favorite dance—the tango—had surprised her.

"'Christmas isn't a season, it's a feeling'", she quoted from her and her mom's favorite movie. "Of course *It's a Wonderful Life*," she added. "It's such a feel-good movie. What about you?"

"*Home Alone*. 'Keep the change, ya filthy animal!'" Rayce laughed at himself. "So I'm juvenile. Sue me. I can relate to the little boy being left home alone."

"You can?" She turned to face him. Relaxed and wrapped in the red-plaid blanket, he seemed like an old friend. It was so easy to sit and talk with him. But his relating to the movie bothered her. An abandoned little boy? And the little drummer boy from his favorite song had been all on his own, too. "Have you been left alone, Rayce?"

"Not like in the movie. My grandparents were always there for me." Behind the couch was a long high table and with a finger he teased the little drummer boy figurine she'd set there.

"Gramps and Grams died when I was in tenth grade. I was…nearly sixteen? I was left alone for weeks after that while the family tried to sort out who would assume guardianship of me. There was only the one aunt in Hawaii and a distant cousin in Europe. Neither were interested in taking in a teenage boy. It was a rough time."

"I can't believe I never knew that in high school. It must have been terribly difficult for your studies."

He shrugged. "I was a jock. Got by on my sports skills and good looks."

"And your devastating charisma, surely. I can't imagine any teacher flunking you after the Rayce Ryan–charm treatment. So who in your family finally decided to take you in?"

"None of them." He chuckled nervously. "When they started talking about child protective services, my coach stepped in. He gave me a room in his basement. I found an apartment after I graduated. By then I was already racing the Master's circuit and had nabbed a few local sponsorships, so I actually had an income to cover basic living expenses. But once I was out of school I moved into full-time competition and the World Cup series. Didn't need much of a place to stay. Just a bed to collapse on after a hard day of training. It's not so bad as it sounds. Don't give me those puppy dog eyes, Cassandra."

"I know training and competition is a full-time job. And you were incredibly lucky to have a coach to take you in. But I suspect living with the coach was more of a business arrangement than getting a replacement family?"

"Yeah, I would have never called Coach Chuck family. At least not when it came to an emotional connection. I don't think it was necessary for the life I was born to live, what with competing and all that."

"Sure, but Rayce, did you have *anyone* to love you?"

He tilted his head. The light that shone through the balcony doors glanced across his eyes, flooding them with a clear sadness. "That's a weird question. What do you mean?"

"Family is there to put their arms around you when you need it. To give you hugs, as you said. To love you."

"My grandparents loved me." He shifted on the couch and propped an elbow to rest his head against his hand. "They were the only parents I've ever known. They raised me because my parents weren't interested in the job after about four months of trying."

"What? Rayce…" Her heart thundering, Cassandra couldn't imagine something so awful. And he explained it with an utter lack of emotion. She immediately thought of what it would be like to never know her parents. Her mom…

"Don't worry, Snow Princess, I had a great childhood. I assumed you knew the story. News media likes to blast all that tragic stuff. It makes for a good lede. But from what my grandparents told me, my parents were hippies who wanted to travel the world in a van and live off the land. They weren't into kids. Something like that. And Grandma always said they showed me the most love by allowing them to raise me."

"So you never knew your parents? Do you see them?"

"Haven't heard from them. Ever. Nor did my grandparents, though I suspect Grandma tried to find them a few times. And after I started hitting the newsstands and had my ugly mug plastered on product displays, I wondered if they'd try to contact me. But no." He shrugged. "Grams and Gramps were the best. When they died, my world was shattered."

"I can't imagine losing them both. At the same time?"

He nodded. "The carbon monoxide detector needed a new battery. They didn't suffer. Passed away in their sleep. I had been away in Denver for a weekend training course."

"Oh, Rayce." She gave his arm a squeeze. "Your heart must have crumbled."

"That's exactly how I felt. And I'm not sure it's ever been put back together in the right way." He took her hand and kissed the back of it. "When I told you I know grief, I meant it."

"So how did you manage such tremendous grief and at such a young age? If you'll share that with me."

"You thinking about your mom?"

She nodded. Tears felt imminent but she fought them back. Now she felt the need to be strong for him, and to listen, to witness the emotional pain he suffered and may have never had opportunity to share with anyone else.

He stroked her hair and the soft touch threatened to make those tears spill. Was he aware of his easy kindness, his genuine concern? If so, that should have filled him with pride.

"I think of them every day," he said. "It used to crush me. But my constant and relentless training schedule forced me to find a place in my heart for them that wouldn't completely send me over the edge. So I put them here." He patted his chest. "I think about them when I need support and guidance. And when I do, I can only smile."

A tear spilled down Cassandra's cheek. "That's lovely. And very strong, especially for a kid who was forced to take care of himself at such a young age. I like that. Finding a place for them in your heart."

She pressed a palm over her own heart. Her mom had always been there. Yet now she felt the hole where she had once been. Could she do the same as Rayce had done? Keep her mom in a compartment that would allow her to move through life without always needing to cry or yell at others because silly things were not right, not "marvelous"?

He touched her cheek to wipe away a tear. "You'll find that ornament," he said. "But if you don't? She's always with you. I promise."

The promise felt real, and it settled into her heart like a warm hug. If Rayce could manage his life and get beyond his grief at such a young age, then surely she was capable of moving forward, too. With or without a silly ornament.

"We got into some deep stuff." He picked up the figurine and gestured with it as he asked, "You okay?"

She nodded. Whew! Even when she had been trying to be strong for him, her heart had stolen that moment to break down.

"Time to change things up. You want to watch a movie?" he asked. "You know I am calling this a date, so a movie generally follows dinner."

His wink seemed to disguise the inner struggle that he'd just revealed to her. Cassandra could feel his yearning desire to change the atmosphere in the room that had gotten heavier with his confession.

Wiping away another tear, she said, "I'm actually exhausted. It's been a long day of business and wrangling of drunk twins. Is it okay if I take a rain check on the movie?"

"Not a problem. I should probably head out. Keep my eyes open for that darn cat while I'm at it, eh?"

"Please do."

"It's been a long time since I've spent such an exceptional evening with a woman."

"Really? I agree it was nice, but it was also… emotional."

"Yeah, sorry about that." He tucked her hair behind her ear. Watching him study her hair and take her in filled her with a heady rush of desire. But acting on that feeling didn't feel right. "Are you going to be okay?"

Always in his presence. "Of course. What about you?"

"Eh… I tend to land on my feet. Usually." He winked. "We're survivors. Even if it doesn't feel that way to you now, you'll rise when the time is right."

The man was charming and outgoing and… always brought out the best in people. But to the detriment of his wounded heart? Was that his means of hiding his pain? His loss? By charming everyone into liking him? Perhaps cockiness was his armor? No, every move he made was genuine.

Standing, she grabbed his hand and walked him to the door. When he pressed his back against it, she felt compelled to make a connection with him. But a kiss didn't feel right. It was too sensual for the mood that lingered over them and with the ghost of her mother haunting her thoughts. And surely he needed some emotional space as well. But the moment demanded touch so…she hugged him. She made it quick, not allowing her body to respond to his warmth, the utter hardness of his muscles, the—

Cassandra stepped out of the hug. "Thanks for a lovely evening."

He marveled at her. "That was nice. We should do it again soon. I mean the date. But also the hug."

"I'm…" always busy and yet, not so busy as she liked to believe she was. Busyness had been her armor. Rayce had loosened it "…free most evenings."

"So am I. And we do live close to one another. Would be a shame if either of us sat alone in our places eating or doing whatever when it could be done with someone we enjoy spending time with."

"A very astute observation. Dinner tomorrow?"

"I'll bring the mistletoe."

CHAPTER NINE

THE SNOWSTORM DISSIPATED in the early morning hours. Snowplows were dispatched and snowcats from all the area's resorts set out on the slopes to groom the runs. Walking paths had to be cleared by hand. Thankfully Cobalt Lake Resort employed a crew of talented interns, whom Cassandra quickly dispatched, shovels in hand.

Fresh snowfall always worked like a beacon as skiers headed out early to enjoy the slopes.

From her balcony overlooking the back patio, Cassandra spied Rayce with his clients. He was an easy spot thanks to his neon-green gear. He'd started wearing the color after contracting with the energy drink. Their logo had been a riot of green splashes. They had also been the first to drop him after his accident. It must have been rough for him. And his coach dropping him while he'd still been in the hospital? That was nothing less than vicious.

Yet there he stood, out on the slopes, trying again. In a different format, but he was doing what he could in the profession he loved. He was not a quitter. His grandparents had raised him right.

That he'd opened up to her last night meant a lot. The information about his teen years, and the loss of the only family he'd known, helped her to understand him better. Despite the obstacles he remained determined.

She glanced to the table behind the couch. The drummer boy figurine was gone. He must have slipped it into a pocket on the way out. It was his totem, she decided, even if he didn't realize it. A boy alone in the world, determined to make his way and give what he had to others.

That day she had fled from him in fear of putting on skis returned to her. Later, when he'd come to her room, he had said something so wise. She would have to step into a pair of skis sooner or later.

Rationally she knew he was right. It wasn't because as the manager of a ski resort she needed to be seen participating in the sport. Rather it was because it had been a part of her life until her mother's death. Skiing felt like breathing. And she did miss it.

But later felt much safer, and more doable, than sooner. Because, when looking down at those skis as Rayce had waited, fear had jittered in her throat like the lump that had settled there that morning she'd learned her mom had been crushed by the avalanche. They'd closed the resort for a week, then finally her dad had made the tough decision that they couldn't risk further lost income, or disappointing guests, and had reopened. The show of support from the Whistler community had been incredible, as well as that from people all over the world. They'd been booked solid through spring, and most guests had sent notes with memories about Cynthia Daniels. It had been heartwarming, but also too much.

Following her mom's death Cassandra had wanted to take some time off. Like a month. But she'd also been aware of her father's pain. He'd lost someone he had loved for twenty-eight years. It would have been selfish of her not to stand by his side and keep the resort running. And her mom would have insisted they do as much. Admittedly last Christmas had been dull and lackluster to the guests. No fabulous Christmas Eve party, or even half the usual decorations.

By clinging to her grief, Cassandra was depriving others of something special. Of their own Christmas memories. Which was the very reason they came to the resort in the first place!

Could she fill the mom-shaped hole in her heart and make it like that place where Rayce kept memories of his grandparents? Always there, but not a heavy weight that overwhelmed her and insisted on keeping her down.

"I can do that," she whispered. "I have to do that."

But how? She already held her mom in her heart. It was the need to cling desperately to her memory that had put her in this funk. She needed to open her fingers, relax her grasp and know that the memories would never flutter away.

And it must start with the daily operations around the resort. She wouldn't allow her grief to interfere with the guests' enjoyment of their vacations. Cassandra decided that with every decoration she hung she would be saying "I love you" to her mom. Even making such a decision seemed to lift the heavy weight from her heart. But a small weight remained.

The missing ornament. How many days had she remaining to find it? A day or two, according to her dad's ultimatum. The email she'd sent to all employees last night to keep an eye out for the ornament had not resulted in a discovery. And every nook and cranny she'd checked only produced another letdown. She needed to resign herself to the idea that it wasn't going to be found. And while it was important to her, what really mattered in the long run was that she remembered making that ornament for her mom and the expression of joy on her face every time she had hung it on the tree.

With a nod and an inhale, she decided today would be a good day. A new day. One that would hold her mom's memory in a special place while also making room for everything else. She would not be a doom-and-gloomer, like Mr. Potter from her favorite Christmas movie.

A knock on the door prompted her to invite Anita inside.

"I brought you a new brew that we're thinking about adding to the menu. It's a creamy chai with lush vanilla bean and a kiss of orange. Really lovely."

"Ooh, sounds intriguing. I love chai." Cassandra inhaled the spices and immediately detected the vanilla.

The sous chef set the tray on Cassandra's desk. On it sat an upside-down cup and a porcelain pot. As usual.

Anita wandered back to the door but paused with her hand holding the door open. "The email said you were looking for an ornament?" she asked. "Did anyone find it?"

"Not yet."

"I will check the kitchen storage," Anita said. "You never know. Odd things end up in there on occasion."

"Thanks, Anita."

After the chef left, Cassandra inhaled the spicy aroma. It made her think of foreign places and exotic fabrics and designs. Someday she'd love to travel to Morocco to see the sights and marvel over the culture. She could manage a week's vacation, especially in the summertime when her dad, ever busy with his many business ventures, enjoyed a break from that busyness and liked to take more control of the daily management of the resort.

Catching sight of a spray of glittery snow from the corner of her eye, she wandered to the patio doors, which were edged with snow. It looked like a frame around a Christmas postcard. Must have been a hunk of snow dropping from the roof.

A flash of neon green caught her attention. Rayce skied slowly beside the Thorson couple. He met with them daily, and each time Cassandra happened to walk near the elderly couple, they regaled her with the ski instructor's kindness and fun manner.

Her dad's idea to hire Rayce had been spoton. But for as much as she felt her heart loosening to allow him into her life, she had to remind herself that he'd only been hired for the season. Come spring he'd be gone. And she did not want to step into any sort of attachment that would eventually be broken. She'd lost too much lately.

Turning to the desk, she followed the spicy scent of chai. Turning over the cup, she gasped, and then laughed. Sitting on the plate was a figurine of a blond kid wearing a Christmas sweater. Upon closer inspection, she realized it was the boy from Rayce's favorite movie.

"Where did he get that? First the little drummer boy and now this guy? I know we don't have this decoration in the resort." Unless it was something one of the employees had brought in? Very possible.

Wherever he'd found it, it made her smile, and laugh when the movie mom's declaration of "Kevin!" struck her thoughts. She tucked the figurine into a pocket then poured the creamy chai. The first sip was amazing. This was definitely going on the menu!

A *ping* on her laptop alerted her. Twelve messages had been forwarded from reception. Good thing she had a pot of chai to get her through the afternoon.

Rayce could see her watching him. From this distance he couldn't quite make out her expression, but a figure dressed in white stood before the patio doors looking in his direction. Heh. She liked him.

More than a few times, as he'd traveled the world by planes, trains and buses, he'd allowed his thoughts to drift back to the good old days of high school, and that beautiful girl he'd always admired. Heck, he'd crushed on her hard. And then she'd run from him.

She wasn't running anymore. Now to get that kiss.

Where *was* he headed with Cassandra? Because it felt like a dating kind of situation. Last night had involved some intense conversation, and stories that he'd never shared with anyone. That stuff had been personal. But he'd felt comfortable opening up to Cassandra. She hadn't made him feel as though he were less than, or wrong for having grown up with a different family structure. And when he'd told her about his grief, it had been real and from the heart.

Yet the last time he'd tossed his heart into the ring, disaster had struck. In the worst way possible. It had robbed him of an Olympic medal. Because the woman he'd thought he loved had kissed another man.

"Stupid heart," he muttered as he glided over the fresh powder toward the Thorsons.

That couple had been married for sixty years! They were respectful and caring toward one another. Man, he'd love to have something like they had. Maybe he should ask for some pointers?

Having clicked out of her skis, Mrs. Thorson lifted a boot for him to loosen the bindings. Rayce knelt before her and made some adjustments.

"You're a good fellow," she said. "You always take your time with us, when you could be out there teaching the youngsters and zipping down the slopes."

"There's no place I'd rather be right now." He set down her boot and stood, only to have Mr. Thorson shake his hand.

"Good stuff, for sure," the old man said.

Rayce lifted his chin. The praise swelled in his chest. It felt like nothing he'd ever experienced on the racing circuit. These two were genuine and honest. They didn't care that he could take the giant slalom in a mere two minutes.

"Tell me your secret," he said to Mr. Thorson. "How have the two of you stayed in love and for so long?" He cast Mrs. Thorson a wink.

Mr. Thorson sat on the bench beside his wife and tilted his bright purple-capped head onto her shoulder. "She's always right. And if you have to go to bed angry, just be sure you're both happy by the morning."

Mrs. Thorson laughed at that seemingly personal comment, while her loving husband hugged her.

Rayce put up his hands in mock dismay. "All

right, you two. Let's keep it safe for the kids. I hear they've got a new hot chocolate flavor with honey and caramel in it over at the nearby stand."

"Ooh." Mrs. Thorson immediately made a beeline for the stand that Rayce had pointed at.

Mr. Thorson slapped him on the shoulder and said, "Just be honest and kind. That's all they want from us." With another wink he went off after his wife.

Honest and kind. Rayce liked that. Simple rules for an amazing marriage.

When he was with Cassandra, their connection felt promising. Her smile. Her laughter. That lush snow-white hair that swept softly across his face when he sat close to her. And the genuine care he recognized in her eyes and her voice. It did things to his stupid heart.

A guy should be more careful. Heck, he was only here for a season. Getting involved would not prove wise. But Rayce Ryan never got anywhere by playing it safe.

Was it love he wanted? Cassandra had seemed worried that he hadn't gotten love in his life. He had. From his grandparents. Familial love. But what might it feel like to fall in love with a woman and to completely abandon his heart to that romantic feeling? Could he do that again? Without fear of injury, rejection or losing the ability to compete?

"Honest and kind," he muttered with a glance toward Cassandra's balcony. She no longer stood there. Was being with Cassandra worth losing his focus?

What *was* worthwhile to him now? If this broken body of his couldn't bring home a gold medal, he'd have to find something to replace his need for adrenaline and competition. The cheers and adoration. The acceptance.

Her absence made his heartbeat stutter.

"Damn it," he whispered. "You're going to go for it, aren't you, stupid heart?"

CHAPTER TEN

A FIRE BLAZED in the outdoor fireplace and the s'mores stand was open for guests. The hot chocolate bar currently offered a dozen different flavors. Cassandra loved the white chocolate cherry version. And who could say no to the dark chocolate and orange spice?

During her rounds she frequently stopped to chat with the guests. But her focus would never be dissuaded. Was the hot chocolate bar clean and inviting? Was the outdoor music set at the right volume? Was all the soot cleared away with not a hint of it on the stone patio? All seemed in order, and the right amount of snow had been heaped behind the cozy chairs. A blanket closet was also heated to provide guests with a comforting wrap of cozy warmth.

"Marvelous," she whispered, hearing the word in her mother's voice.

Yes, Mom, it is marvelous. And...with or without an ornament, I can keep you close. I can do this. I can move beyond the grief. I am capable of changing...

"What's that?"

Spinning around and landing in Rayce's arms, Cassandra felt a brief effusion of joy that was quickly replaced by decorum. "Rayce, I didn't see you behind me."

"Keeping you on your toes. That's my job. So, what's marvelous?"

"Oh, nothing really. And everything. Well, not everything. It's what I strive for," she explained as she began to walk the path and he accompanied her.

A trip completely around the lake wasn't necessary but she did like to walk up to the first observation point to do a scan and make sure all the lights were working.

"You strive for marvelous," he recited. "Sounds unattainable."

"It's something my mom used to say. She was very fussy. Everything has a place and position. She would spend hours daily going through the resort, making it look perfect. The guests expected it."

"So that's where you got your need for perfection."

"There's nothing wrong with wanting the best and creating a memorable experience for others."

"Fair enough. So marvelous is the ultimate goal?"

"Absolutely. And...I think I've come close this year with the decorations. I just want to make my mom proud." She clasped her hands before her mouth briefly. "But that ornament."

"I can help you look some more?"

Once at the observation point, he stopped alongside her and leaned his elbows onto the banister where guests could walk out and gaze over the lake in the summer. The bench seating had been recently swept and weatherproof seat cushions were neatly placed in a cubicle for guests to use. While there wasn't an attendant posted, there was an abundance of treats in a small cabinet to satisfy any snack attacks.

"After our chat last night, I had a talk with myself about letting it go," she confessed.

"How's that going?"

A heavy sigh felt like a mutiny of her determination. "Letting it go is... It's become this *thing* that I need to clutch or accomplish or even defeat. I don't know how else to put it."

"You mean, letting go of the thing that connects you to your mom? And you'll never reach that particular marvelous if you don't find the ornament?"

She hadn't thought of it quite that way, but he was spot-on. She nodded and bowed her head.

That he understood her always surprised her. He wasn't the unattainable golden boy she'd once put on a pedestal. Rayce seemed so normal, not like the celebrity persona he'd embraced with open arms. Had the accident brought him down or was it that he was new here and hadn't found his footing yet? Maybe the real Rayce Ryan would rise soon enough.

"So, what are we doing out here?" he asked. "Beyond listening to Elvis croon about Christmas?"

"Making the evening rounds before I turn in. One final check for—"

"Marvelous?"

"You got it. Let's walk back but take the path around the fireplace so I can check on the shoveling situation to the employee cabins."

"I can tell you right now it's all good, but I suspect you need to see it to believe it. I don't mind." He stretched out an arm, his hand open in invitation. "You can walk me home."

He winked at her and clasped her hand. She was wearing thin gloves and he wasn't. Never had she wanted to rip them off more than now to feel his warmth, the sureness of his skin against hers. When had she last walked with a man and held his hand? Such a silly thought, yet it was something that went beyond mere friendship. So...why not?

Tugging from his grasp, she bit the finger of her glove and pulled it off, tucking them both in her pocket. When she clasped his hand again, she said, "Much better."

He gave her hand a squeeze. "You always have been the smart one."

Smart, or rather hungry for his warmth and the feel of his skin against hers?

"How's the coaching going?" she asked.

"Better than expected. I really want to take Mr. and Mrs. Thorson home with me when this gig is over."

"They are a sweet couple. Oh. Do they remind you of your grandparents?"

"Maybe? They're just good, fun people. Honest and kind."

"Those are the best sorts of people."

"They make me think. A lot."

"About what?"

He jumped ahead onto the first wide log step that led upward to the employee cabins. It was well-swept and edged with bright strip lighting to prevent accidents in the dark.

"I don't know," he said. "Just life and love and things like that." He dashed up a few more of the massive log steps and she followed. When he pulled her to him, her heart leaped. "You're easy to be around, and that is a new experience for me. I like you, Cassandra."

It felt as though he were declaring his love for her, but she wasn't so foolish as to believe that. It was a delicious feeling, though, to hear that from him.

"You make me feel less broken. Come inside," he said with a gesture toward his cabin. "For a few minutes?"

Unable and unwilling to conjure a quick excuse, Cassandra nodded and followed him down a shoveled pathway to the small single-room cabin.

That word he'd spoken swiftly and softly—*broken*—disturbed her. Is that what he thought of himself? She supposed it was inevitable after what he'd been through. But it put an ache in her very soul to hear his confession.

Before following him inside, she heard a *meow* and turned to spy the white cat scampering across the path they'd taken.

"Is it that darned cat?" Rayce asked.

"Yes, but he darted away. I told the grounds crew to keep an eye out and catch it," she said, closing the door behind her. "Surely, someone would like to adopt the thing. It's so fluffy."

Rayce shrugged off his jacket and tossed it to the couch, but it missed and landed on the floor. "I haven't gotten groceries yet, but I do have snacks and beer. Want a bottle?"

Cassandra picked up his coat and carefully laid it over the back of the couch. "Sure."

He handed her an icy bottle of craft beer from a local brewery. "Have a seat."

She sat on the couch, finding it surprisingly comfy. When she was little, she'd followed her mom from cabin to cabin, helping her to straighten things out, take inventory and order new pillows and linens when necessary. All she could recall was bouncing on this couch, never actually sitting in it like a normal person.

"I know, right?" he said as he settled onto the couch beside her and put his feet up on the coffee table fashioned by a local artist who used fallen lumber rescued from the forest. "It conforms nicely and embraces you like a hug without being under-stuffed and uncomfortable."

"Wow. I just learned who the resident couch connoisseur is."

"When you spend your late teen years couch surfing, you develop a talent." He tilted his bottle against hers. "To big comfy couches and good conversation."

"What did you want to talk about?"

"Anything and everything, as long as it's with you. We've done the favorite things." Head tilted against the back of the couch, he turned his gaze to her. His summer sky eyes caught her instantly. Could a woman ever tire of staring into them?

"Tell me something I don't know that no one would guess about you."

Cassandra considered that one as she sipped. "I'm not so fussy as I appear."

"Doubt it," he countered. "You couldn't let my coat stay on the floor."

"That's aesthetics. I'm a terrible mess in the bathroom. I leave towels on the floor, beauty supplies sitting everywhere."

"You're an absolute heathen." He chuckled. "Come on, give me something good."

"Like what? We've both shared our grief. Hmm, what about a true confession that doesn't involve a family member? Just about you. Personally."

"Fair enough."

He shifted to face her and she danced her gaze over his face. He had mastered the sexy stubble and finger-combed hair. No wonder he'd been on every magazine cover; the man gave good face.

"I'm not good at recognizing emotion," he finally said. "I mean, stuff like love and anger and indifference."

"Really? I would think anger an easy one."

"You'd think, but I've walked into more fights than you can imagine. People tell me I'm too easygoing. I like to joke and prod at people. It's a means of pushing them out of their comfort zones. I think I picked it up from Coach. He was always pushing me to see what I was capable of. Guess it makes me kind of one way or the other."

"I don't understand."

He shrugged. "Things are always either too far to the left or right. Too good or too bad. It's rare that I'm balancing in the middle. It's what I know. I'd like to be in the middle more often. To be more balanced."

"But I thought you enjoyed competing? The challenge. That must weigh heavily to the good."

"Actually it weighs on both sides. Competition is rough stuff."

"That's probably what trained your brain for those two extremes. I wouldn't think the middle ground would satisfy you."

"Right? But, well…" He let out a heavy sigh. "It's something I need to explore. After spending half my life in the extremes, I wonder what I've missed. Can I be a normal guy?"

"I don't think you'll ever qualify as normal, and I wouldn't want you to be so. You're too interesting, Rayce."

He leaned in closer and fluttered his lashes at her. "I think you like me, Snow Princess."

"Of course I like you."

"Do you like me enough to kiss me?"

Her mouth dropped open. Cassandra quickly closed it. And the first words out of her mouth were, "Where's that mistletoe?"

He dug in his back pocket and produced the plastic frond, which was growing crumbled and bent.

"Do you carry that everywhere?"

"If there's one thing I've learned over the years, it's to always be prepared."

"Scouts?"

"No, it's the 'not being willing to get the seat next to the bathroom if I'm late for the bus, train, or plane' kind of preparedness training."

Her laughter escaped in a burst and when she came down from it, Rayce met her with a kiss. Their skin still slightly chilled from the outside air, their initial connection caused a deliciously cool spark. It ignited and shivered through her system, quickly racing through her body to awaken all nerve endings. The crowd cheering in her head was really the thrill of her soul dancing to this moment.

Finally, it shouted. *That kiss you regret walking away from is finally yours.*

As they deepened the kiss, Rayce slid a hand along her cheek and cupped the back of her head. It wasn't tentative or shy. They had connected. And the intensity of the moment surprised her. He knew how to move and met her with an initial softness that then became a little firmer, even daring. Yes, he dared to go deeper, to draw her in closer, to defy her to push him away. Of course she should expect nothing less from the man who was determined to shake up her world.

There wasn't an excuse in existence that would tempt her to push him away.

Reaching up, she glided her fingers through his hair. It was just as soft as she'd imagined it would be. The move pressed them even closer and she laughed a little as they tilted their heads to reconnect differently. The sudden rush of heated passion brewed the moment into a delicious and electric embrace.

As quickly as she had fallen into the joyous surrender, he pulled back and smiled at her.

"No audience," he whispered, with a dart of his eyes to illustrate their quiet surroundings. "It was a long wait, but I'm glad it finally happened."

"I am, too." Giddy swirls spun through her system. Her shallow breaths came as fast as her heartbeats. "I think…one more."

Gripping him by the sweater, she pulled him to her. This kiss was the one she'd craved for years. The one she'd regretted never accepting. The one she'd always wondered about when kissing anyone else. The one she would never refuse. This kiss melded them in a clasp of desire that she wasn't about to destroy by running from it.

But as well, this kiss answered her deep need for connection. For that hug she'd been missing.

For an intimacy that fed her soul in a surprising manner, that went beyond mere attraction.

Rayce bowed his forehead to hers. "Something has started here."

Really? Because she was wont to believe that it had started a long time ago. At least in her heart.

"Another?" he asked.

She nodded.

They'd learned one another's mouths and moved quickly to kisses that were deep and long and, oh, so satisfying. And when the hand he had pressed against her back moved around to caress her breast, Cassandra arched forward against his body, wanting...

So much. And yet how dare she take such pleasure when she should be focusing on other things like honoring her mother by making the tree marvelous through the addition of the ornament? She had intended to get that settled before losing herself in a relationship.

Relationship? Why was she even *thinking* that word?

Breaking the kiss, she stood and tugged down her sweater. "I gotta go. Sorry. I'm... This... can't go any further tonight."

"Okay. Yeah. Sorry. That was moving a little fast."

"Just a little." She grabbed her coat on the way to the door.

When she gripped the doorknob, she bowed her head. She was attracted to Rayce. Her entire body screamed for more, more and more! And she wasn't so precious that she wouldn't allow herself to get involved with the man simply because he was an employee. It was her life; she could do as she pleased. And she did crave intimate contact with his naked body, the ultimate deepening of their connection.

"It's not what you want," he called from behind her. "I'm sorry. I was going to be smarter about romance. I think my stupid heart has overstepped."

Smarter about romance? His stupid heart? No, it wasn't stupid. It was being cautious. He'd been through so much in his lifetime. And they understood one another on the grief front. But this side of their relationship was—not so much a challenge as a step in a new direction for her. She wasn't sure what she wanted from Rayce. Or rather she did want something from him— body contact, his hand on her thigh, his mouth on hers—and she didn't know how to take it. Would it be fair to only take that from him without committing to something more?

Oh, she didn't want to talk now. She needed to be alone to sort out her feelings about him.

"It's not you, Rayce. See you tomorrow," she called, then closed the door.

At the bottom of the log staircase, she paused and turned back to the cabin. Soft downy snowflakes fluttered before her. She'd fled from him once again. And this time, she felt even more confused by her conflicting emotions. What did grief over her mother have to do with allowing Rayce into her heart? Surely she had room for both of them there? And since he'd arrived at Cobalt Lake Resort, she'd relaxed her staunch work habits and begun to enjoy herself.

So why the escape from what could have turned into a heavy-duty make-out session? The man could kiss! And she had waited ten years for him. Not that she'd stood around waiting. No, she thought she'd never see Rayce again after high school. But the fact that he was back in her life, in a surprisingly intimate way, made her flush warmer than a sip of hot chocolate.

Rayce had been right about one thing. She did reach uncomfortable quickly. She shouldn't have fled.

Was it too late to turn and go back inside?

"It is," she whispered.

Returning to Rayce's embrace would stir up a new conversation that would involve going deeper into her heart than she could manage right now.

CHAPTER ELEVEN

BRAD DANIELS CHATTED with the electrician who had stopped in to go over the resort's electricals with him. The twosome shook hands and he directed the man to take off on his own—he knew the building—then turned to face Cassandra.

"Dad, how's the wiring and all that important electrical jazz?"

"Just jazzy," he replied with a killer smile that always seemed to turn the heads of the female guests. But the addition of jazz hands went a bit too far.

Cassandra clasped her hands over his to make it stop. "Fair enough."

"So now we can flick on the Christmas tree lights."

"Uh…" She had been coaching herself to move beyond her grief and accept she may never find the ornament, but her heart still hadn't quite gotten the memo. Last night's desperate escape from the arms of a sexy man who had only wanted to get closer to her was proof of that.

Her dad's gaze switched from the massive, beautifully decorated tree, back to her. "The electrician said there's nothing wrong with the remote or any of the connections. It's the big welcome to the resort."

"Yes, but I still haven't found Mom's ornament. And I do have a day or two left on your ultimatum."

"Right. I forgot about that." He shrugged. "Maybe it's already on the tree. Got stuffed deep inside on a pine bow somewhere?"

Did he have no idea which one it was? Or how much it meant to her?

"No, I looked."

He rubbed his salt-and-pepper stubbled jaw. "It's just an ornament, Cassie. Don't you want the guests to *ooh* and *aah* over the fabulous lights? Your mother would appreciate that more than some silly little ornament."

"It's not silly!"

Startled at her outburst, her dad initially cringed, then he pulled her to him for a hug. As much as she didn't want anyone to witness such a moment, Cassandra's body leaned into the much-needed hug and she tilted her head onto his shoulder. The sudden rise of endorphins coursing through her body switched from manic anger to a soothing stream of comfort. Her dad was her rock, the man who had held her hand at the funeral and promised her she would survive, that they both would.

"I know you miss her, Cassie," he said with a kiss to the top of her head. "I think of her every day."

That was the same thing Rayce had said, that he'd thought of his grandparents every day. Was it easier for men to move on? No, that sounded ridiculous. Obviously her dad finding new love had helped immensely on the *moving on* front.

"But you've started a new life with Faith."

"I thought you were happy about Faith?"

The two had gotten engaged after a whirlwind romance. They had known one another from high school and reconnected after years apart. And Cassandra did approve of Faith. She was kind, smart and independent enough to not take any of her dad's nonsense. Not that he had an ounce of it in his bones, but he did have his trying moments.

A bit like Rayce and his needing to push her. Hmm... Was she attracted to a man who reminded her of her dad? Nothing wrong with that, especially since Brad Daniels was one of the best.

"I am happy that you're happy, Dad. I just... I'm moving slower than expected on this whole 'letting Mom go' thing, I guess."

"You don't ever have to let her go, sweetie.

She's still right here." He patted his heart. "Got a nice little nest where she resides."

Cassandra spread her fingers over his chest, feeling his heartbeat, and imagining her mom so close. She felt much the same when things were just right—*marvelous*, as her mother would grandly announce. And Rayce had placed his grandparents in the same manner, right there, in his heart. It was beautiful. She could do the same…

"Give me another day to find the ornament," she asked more than told him. "It's…" She sighed. A weird, ineffable thing she honestly couldn't put into words.

"I get it. But think of our guests. And, you know your mother would not be happy to see the tree lights dark."

He was right: Cynthia Daniels *would* be upset about the dark tree. "One more day." Cassandra held up a fist and he met her in agreement with a fist bump.

"All right, I have to find Faith. She's convinced we need to start wedding planning sooner rather than later. Fancy invitations to order. Silly colors to pick out."

"Have fun with it, Dad."

"Speaking of fun, how's Rayce working out?"

"With the job?"

"Uh, yes? Is there anything else I'd be wondering about? Like maybe the fact that I saw you two walking the path last night? Hand in hand."

Oh, bother, and here she'd thought they'd been all alone and unwatched. But they hadn't kissed outside. Nothing to give her dad reason to suspect they were anything but friends. Except the hand-holding.

"I like him, Dad. Both as a professional ski instructor who has been getting rave reviews from our guests and…"

He put an arm around her shoulder. "Anything that makes your face light up and your eyes sparkle is okay in my book. Maybe we'll have a double wedding, eh?"

"Oh, please, Dad, we're just…"

What *were* they? What did she want them to be? During their make-out session last night, she'd abruptly fled Rayce's cabin. By the time she'd returned to her apartment, she decided it had been nerves.

But she couldn't get what Rayce had said out from her thoughts: *I was going to be smarter about romance.* And he was always calling his heart stupid. What did that mean? It couldn't reflect well on her if his heart had chosen her in a moment of stupidity.

"I have to run, actually." She tapped her watch that blinked with a reminder. "I've got an appointment for…something or other. Talk later, Dad!"

She left swiftly, with her dad's chuckles trailing in her wake. He knew exactly what she hadn't been able to put into words. That she and Rayce were more than simply friends.

And when she considered it, she did want more from Rayce. But she wouldn't label them boyfriend and girlfriend. And certainly not lovers. Taking things slowly was all right by her. But it was not knowing how Rayce felt about the two of them that would drive her mad with wonder.

She owed him an explanation for her quick retreat last night. And with hope, he'd let her a little further into his psyche so she could understand what sort of challenge Rayce Ryan's stupid heart presented to her wanting soul.

Standing at the top of one of the medium challenge runs, Rayce's thoughts were on the snow princess whom he'd kissed last night. Three kisses actually. He had been counting. But then he'd gotten cocky and made a move that was too fast for her. He'd scared her off.

"Not cool." He needed to be more respectful of her needs and…desires.

Never before had he been so cognizant of his actions, of how one wrong move might destroy something he wanted with increasing desire. He must follow Cassandra's lead. It felt like the right way to proceed with her. She required patience, honesty and kindness. Just like he needed the proverbial pat on the back.

He'd grown up knowing that unless he performed a skill perfectly, the pat would not be forthcoming. And…he didn't get them anymore. Not in the form of a coach nodding their approval, the cheer of an audience as they watched him speed by or even the flash of paparazzi cameras as he smiled for the fans.

Life had been so focused, and yes, rushed. If he hadn't been training, skiing or traveling with his coach, he was listening to performance audio tapes and practicing various martial arts to maintain a level of flexibility and skill that was unparalleled by his opponents. Always his eyes had been on the prize. Take a photo with the ribbon, medal or fake gold cup. On to the next event. Not a moment to savor his accomplishments. Not when he had to best himself the next race by a tenth of a second.

Now any chance of earning such pride had been stripped away, leaving him but a man who had lost a dream and who wasn't certain how to move forward.

Life had changed the moment he'd crashed out of the Olympics. And in what had seemed like a split second, all the fans turned to look at the other guy, the newest Alpine racing sensation. The cameras had ceased their blinding flashes in his direction. And even the media, after the routine interviews in the hospital about the pitiful damaged skier, had tucked away their interest and moved on. Along with Coach Chuck. Rayce had never considered Coach a replacement grandparent, or any kind of family member, but he had been his mentor and guide and influenced his every move for so long.

While the cameras and attention had seemed to fill him up at the time, now he realized he did not miss the frenzy, the surface adoration and the false worship that had come along with it. None of it had been real. It was all a show. And he'd been the star of that show for a short time.

But if he didn't feel the innate pull to put on another show, what came next? Race, crash, recover, repeat had been his mantra throughout his competition years. He didn't feel compelled to *repeat* now. And that wasn't as alien a feeling as it should be.

Because lately, when he was with Cassandra, he experienced a different but similar feeling to the racing euphoria. Acceptance. Importance. Not being judged, but rather feeling he could fill the space and simply exist alongside her and she would make him feel like he had done something right.

Cassandra made him feel like he was a little less broken.

It was a feeling he wanted to chase, to inhale and absorb like oxygen into his muscles. But he didn't want to make a mistake and risk crashing out of what they had started. This could be something, and he had to recognize that and honor it without being thrown for a loop by the woman. And sacrificing his stupid heart.

"It is stupid," he muttered. "It's not smart enough to know what's real and what is just a game."

Cassandra didn't play games. Yet her abrupt departure last night after those amazing kisses had tugged at his softening heart, pulling it to a stretch until it snapped back with a sting. She hadn't wanted to remain in his cabin one moment longer. Had he done something wrong? He'd thought she'd wanted that kiss as much as he had.

Stabbing a ski pole into the snow, he flipped down his goggles. Here behind a line of trees, no one at Cobalt Lake Resort who happened to be standing out on their balcony could see him. Rayce didn't need Cassandra to see him; this was about proving to himself that he could do this.

With an inhale, he stretched his back. The twinge of pain didn't bite too sharply. And his leg wasn't bothering him at all. Excellent. He wasn't going to slow this one down. He needed to push himself, to test his limits.

Pushing off, Rayce tucked his poles back and his body bent and lowered to minimize resistance. The slap of the brisk winter air on his cheeks was the best thing in the world. Icy and biting yet burning a heat flash in its wake. A shift of his weight took the gentle curve and then he headed into a swift schuss toward the bottom.

Yes! This felt like his old normal. Free and always racing downward and striving for a goal. The goal right now? Make it to the bottom in one piece.

Laughing at his thoughts, he neared the base of the slope and…his thigh muscle twinged. Fear gripped his senses and his body tilted. His ski angled at the same time as a volt of pain strafed up his spine. A fall was imminent.

Knowing how to take a fall, Rayce readied himself. He landed against the snowbank at the edge of the run in a graceless collapse and roll that spat up sprays of snow. His body settled lying on his back, face up, skis splayed and feet turned outward.

No one around to see that beautiful disaster, thankfully.

"Idiot," he muttered and pounded the snow with both fists. His hip burned. Pain scattered up and down his spine with sharp prickles that made him grit his teeth. "You think you can compete again?"

Who was he kidding? He'd never again be as effortlessly fearless on skis as he once was. He gritted his teeth and eased his fingers over the cramping thigh muscles. A reminder of what he had done to himself. Through emotional stupidity. One moment of self-absorption had cost him so much.

Rayce swore and slapped the packed snow. In truth? It wasn't that he *couldn't* do this; he simply *didn't want* to do this. He'd had a good run. Time to move on.

Because his life had changed.

Staring up at the icy blue sky, his breaths condensing before him, he recalled what Cassandra had said about her mother. Cynthia Daniels had triggered an avalanche. These mountains were dangerous. And with the ocean so near, the weather could change faster than a snap of fingers. Even the most experienced skiers risked death by a sudden avalanche. It would be an awful way to go. Buried alive. If it ever happened to him, he prayed his lungs would be crushed by the incredible weight of the snow, instantly taking his life.

Cassandra must have been inconsolable in the days following her mother's death, just as he had been when he'd learned about his grandparents' demise. Grandpa had been meaning to buy a carbon monoxide detector for over a year. Following that dreadful news, he'd wanted to skip training. Coach Chuck had given him a week, then convinced him training was the best thing for his mental health. And his grandparents would be proud to know he hadn't given up.

Coach had known all the right things to say. And yet... Would Rayce have been better off if he'd taken a little longer to mourn and grieve the loss of the two most important people in his life? There were days he wished he would have, but honestly he could never know if it would have changed his future in any way. Coach had been insistent he return to training. But when things had come down to the wire, Coach had revealed his true colors in the hospital after Rayce's crash.

"You screwed up," Coach Chuck had said. The man's severe, unemotional tone was as clear as a bell in Rayce's memory. It was the foul language—something Coach had never used—that had shocked Rayce. "All that work. And for what?"

Coach hadn't stopped by again after that admonishment. And when Rayce finally called him, the man said he needed to step back. Give Rayce some room.

Rayce hadn't realized it at the time, but it had

been Coach Chuck's way of dodging a bad situation. And of accepting a younger skier under his tutelage that he'd been talking to for a year and hadn't mentioned to Rayce. He'd learned about that from the media.

And now who was left in this world to care for Rayce Ryan?

He sat up and stabbed a pole into the snow. He hadn't twisted his ankle. He'd fallen correctly. He'd just feel a little sore for a while. Feeling sorry for himself was more stupid than throwing a race because he'd seen his girlfriend kissing another man.

Cassandra would never use his heart in such a cruel manner. She was true and kind, if a little perfectionist. But he liked that about her. And she gave him the emotional connection he'd lost following the accident. Or possibly it was a connection he hadn't felt since his grandparents were alive.

Who do you have to love you?

That was the real question, wasn't it? He'd succeeded in kissing The Girl He Could Never Have. Now, to trust his heart and follow it to the end? Or would he let her down as he seemed to let down everyone who had ever walked into his life?

CHAPTER TWELVE

NIGHT HAD FALLEN and the view from Cassandra's balcony boasted a fairyland of sparkles and colored lighting. The fireplace below had coaxed out dozens of guests despite the falling snow. It was that big fluffy, soft stuff that looked like goose down and she would swear to anyone that it tasted like candy.

It had been a while since she'd caught a snowflake on her tongue. Wrapping the chenille blanket tighter around her shoulders, she remained on the balcony watching the guests. And when a snowflake fluttered closer, within reach—a knock at her door startled her from catching it.

With a frown she padded inside to answer the door. Her thick knitted calf-high slippers with rubber grips on the soles made squidgy noises on the gleaming hardwood floor. She never expected anyone after ten in the evening so it could only be...

"Rayce."

He tossed and caught the plastic mistletoe a

few times. The man was a master of the easy yet cocky smile. But that smile dropped when he noticed her expression. "Really? Is that disappointment? Way to make a man feel welcome, Snow Princess."

"No, it's not. Come in!"

"Are you sure? Because your face—" he gestured before her face with the mistletoe "—is saying something different."

She tugged him across the threshold, then led him through the living room to the open balcony door. "I was standing outside, trying to catch snowflakes on my tongue when you interrupted me."

"Oh." Seeming reassured he hadn't been the problem, he stood on the threshold. "And here I thought you were over me after last night."

"No, I—" They'd have the conversation about her fleeing him, but first things first. "Grab a blanket from the couch and join me!"

A moment later he stood shoulder to shoulder with her, blankets cozily wrapped about them. He leaned over the railing, tongue thrust out.

"It's not as easy as it looks," he said.

Cassandra tilted back her head and opened her mouth. Snowflakes *plished* on her forehead. A cool one melted on her nose. And… "Yes!" It melted on her tongue with a sweet kiss of winter. "I love that flavor."

"What flavor is that?" Rayce pulled her close and she hugged against him.

"The flavor of childhood," she decided. "I haven't tasted a snowflake in that long. It's a good memory."

"I'll remember that next time I do a face-plant in the powder."

She laughed. "I suppose you eat snow all the time, like it or not."

"I've consumed more than a man should, and never voluntarily. Maybe even recently—"

"Did you fall?"

"Eh… Took a stumble. Sometimes the ole leg…" He sighed. "We're not feeling sorry for ourselves tonight. So, can I see if the flavor of a snowflake still lingers on your tongue?"

Their gazes dropped to mouths and with a nod, she leaned in to meet his lips with hers. The winter kiss started with the sweet nip of chill, which quickly warmed. The change in temperature at their mouths was framed by the cool air, the hush of snowflakes dusting their faces and hair. *Magical* was an easy word to describe the moment. Maybe even… No, it couldn't possibly be… *Marvelous?*

"Kissing you is better than tasting snowflakes," he said against her mouth.

"I agree." She pulled him in for another kiss that could melt snowflakes in an instant. Was it possible to achieve the ultimate approval in a kiss?

Rayce's kiss lured her closer and she snuggled against his chest. He opened his blanket and she spread her hands around his back, as he did at her waist. His touch burned in the best way, warming her faster than the fire below. There was a certain perfection to their embrace that defied logic. He was the opposite of her, wild and cocky and a seeker of attention; she preferred the background and order and yet wasn't afraid to share herself when the moment was right. Like now. Rayce brought out things in her she had always known were there, but hadn't seen much of recently. Like passion and curiosity.

With a nuzzle of his nose along her cheek, he slid away the hair from her neck and glided a kiss to her earlobe. Erotic shivers tickled from her neck, over her scalp and down to her toes. Yet they stood outside on the balcony. Anyone below who looked up…

Rayce's hair was capped with white. She brushed off the snowflakes. "It's starting to pick up. Let's go inside."

Both shook out their blankets before going inside. "I want to check out that massive fireplace one of these days," Rayce said. "There's always a lot of people huddled around it."

"Making s'mores and singing Christmas carols. So did you just stop by to kiss me?" Cassandra asked as she wandered to the kitchen to see what she had for wine or beer. A half bottle of red? It would serve. She grabbed two goblets and joined him on the couch. "Sorry. Leftovers."

"That's fine. Maybe I did come over just for a kiss," he said. "Or two. Or three?"

She clinked her goblet against his. "I'm in for three. I saw you this morning standing out on the Harmony run."

"Yeah? You can't keep your eyes off me, can you?"

"It was the glare from your ski visor that caught my attention. But…I admit you're not so terrible to look at."

"You say that as if a forced confession. Who's holding a knife to your throat, Snow Princess?"

"Sorry." Over a sip of wine she met his gaze. Using her best sultry tone she said, "You're very handsome. How's that?"

"And?"

"And? A great kisser. And very…"

He lifted a brow, awaiting her summation.

"Annoying, actually." She moved aside and poked him in the thigh. "What is that sharp thing? Seriously? You carry that mistletoe with you everywhere."

"It's my good luck mistletoe. Hey, my mistletoe maneuver got me another kiss."

"Have you ever used it on anyone else?"

"Never." He made a show of crossing his heart with a finger. "Promise. There's not a woman in this world who could lure this mistletoe above her head, except you."

He tugged the pitiful thing from his pocket and adjusted the wired branches but there was no saving the crumbled tangle of green plastic leaves and fake white berries. "I bet the real stuff would get me—"

Cassandra choked on a sip of wine. "Would get you what?"

They stared at one another as the silence caressed them with an intimate tension. She suspected he would have said *in bed*. And guilt did shade his expression. Though she suspected there wasn't a lewd comment in this world that would make Rayce Ryan blush.

Nothing wrong with expecting they move to the next level of intimacy. That kiss on the balcony had certainly stoked something inside her. Sleeping together was not off the table. Especially on a night like this. Cold outside but cozy inside. Goose down flakes falling softly from the sky. And moonlight enhancing it all.

"I didn't mean…" he started.

"I know what you meant. And you don't need real mistletoe to get that, either."

His brow quirked. On the other hand he wasn't

going to be here forever. And she'd flinched the other night when his hand strayed, seeking a more intimate connection. And yet on the other, borrowed, hand she was a big girl. She could do what she wanted.

"Rayce, why are you tiptoeing around me? We can have sex like two adults if we want to."

"I… Right. Of course we can. I just…" He spread his arms across the back of the couch and put up his feet on the coffee table. "Well, you kind of ran away from me last night."

"Because you implied you were doing the dating thing wrong."

"I didn't—oh. Right. Don't take it personally, Cassandra. It's my stupid heart."

"I don't understand why you keep calling your heart stupid. It doesn't reflect well if it was stupid enough to kiss me."

"Kissing you is not stupid, Cassandra. That's the best thing in the world. I'm sorry." He shrugged. "I say that because my heart tends to get me in trouble. Big trouble. And I want to be careful with it. Not follow it too closely into danger."

"All this interaction between us, the dinners and romance, and the utilization of mistletoe, involves some risk. Danger, as you put it."

"I know." He took her hand and kissed the back of it. Summer sky eyes met hers over the top of her hand. How could he possibly believe danger was involved in their interactions? "This is different, Cassandra. I want to do everything right."

"Does my need for perfection prompt that?"

"Nope. I find that part of you adorable. It's... I really like you. And I don't want to send you running."

"Have you had many women run from you?"

"My stupid heart will never tell. Listen, Cassandra, some truths here? I'm not a big dater."

"Seriously? Because every time I've opened a magazine or scrolled online these past few years, I usually saw you with your arm around a woman."

"The rags! Half the time those dates were set up. Makes for good press."

"But what about the Grammys? I distinctly recall seeing you with Aliana Garnet."

"Ah, the infamous 'leaning in' pic that surfaced online and the whole world thought I was kissing her. In reality, we'd been set up for the evening. We didn't click. At all. She smelled like fancy perfume and the scent made me dizzy. And I was too short for her, even though I was inches taller. Those crazy high heels she was wearing! Anyway, that photo was taken when I was whispering something to her about needing to find a bathroom."

Cassandra laughed. "Really?"

"Hey, when a guy's gotta go... Aliana was

not at all impressed with me. I didn't even score a kiss. Not that I wanted one. That *date*—" he crimped his fingers in air quotes "—was all for show. She should have thanked me, though. Her TikTok numbers soared. And I'm pretty sure I scored the *Rolling Stone* interview because of it."

"So it was a…business date?"

"Exactly. Super boring. Both of us were working the angles, making sure it served our own bottom lines. Admittedly I have had a few real girlfriends that I thought cared about me, and in turn I cared about them. But nothing that ever lasted. You may have noticed I have a big ego. If I'm not the star, then no one else can be. At least that's what one of them shouted while she was throwing shoes at me and telling me to leave her place. I caught one and took it with me. She texted me to return it, but…I can be a jerk sometimes."

Sounds like the woman may have deserved the theft if she had been throwing things at him. On the other hand there was always two sides to every story.

"Then why the job here at the resort?" she asked. "Seems insignificant for a man of your ego. The media are not allowed, and you're never going to get your photo on social media for being seen coaching an octogenarian couple on the bunny hill."

"Isn't that the truth! Honestly? This job was

all that was offered to me. After the accident I lost my endorsements and the whole world forgot I existed. My manager tried to find me some action but other than a few movie roles—"

"Movie roles? Why didn't you take those?"

"I am not an actor. And I don't need the money. I've saved a good portion from my endorsement deals. And one thing I can do is invest wisely. I'm set for life."

"That's good to know. I'd hate to think you were destitute. What about the fame and attention? I know you miss that."

Letting out a hefty exhale, Rayce toyed with the blanket that he'd tossed across his lap. "I do like the attention. Crave it. But…"

"But?"

"I don't know." He scruffed his fingers through his hair. "I've only been at the resort a little while and have worked with some interesting guests. I was thinking about it as I lay at the bottom of Harmony."

"You were *lying* on the slope?"

"Had a minor misstep. My leg is intent on reminding me I'll never get back to racing form."

"Rayce, you have to be careful."

"Don't worry about me. Besides, I wear that GPS tracker badge when I'm out there. Resort rules, don't you know."

"Those trackers give me and my dad peace of

mind. We've had to utilize them more than a few times."

"They are smart. But as for me and Cobalt Lake Resort, I like the smallness of it. The slower pace and personal attention and taking my time to show someone how to do something right. Don't get me wrong. If I sensed a camera within smiling distance, I'd slap on a grin and pose. That's nutty, isn't it? What's wrong with me, Cassandra? I don't want to be that guy who needs validation from others to exist."

"Seems like you're taking a step in a direction that may not require such validation. If you're enjoying the coaching?"

"Watching Mr. and Mrs. Thorson take their first run down the hill was a hoot. They even clasped hands. It was cute. And, I don't know, it made me…feel."

"Feel like what?"

"Just feel."

"Oh."

It was half sad and half good to hear him say that. Had the man never experienced the joy of helping others? Of being validated simply for existing and not because he'd accomplished a task or won an event?

"You think I'm a nutjob. I can see it in your eyes."

She touched his jaw. The thick stubble enhanced the sensory appeal. Rugged on the outside yet a bit softer on the inside. Rayce Ryan did not cease to surprise her. And that he shared those complicated parts of himself with her meant so much. And yet...

"I'm a little sad that you haven't had moments of validation outside of your sport," she said.

"I have. My grandparents were loving and kind and always there to cheer me on. Even if it was walking in the Sunday school parade dressed like an Easter lamb. Life changed a lot after they passed. I don't know if I can ever get back to that place of comfort and love." He exhaled. "Will I ever have a family? Someone to care about me? Can I ever have a real home?"

"Rayce, you are worthy of all that and more. And you'll find your family, people who care about you. You've had a rough time of it this past...well, probably all during your competition years."

"I wouldn't call challenging myself rough. The physical part of it was awesome. It's that emotional stuff that baffles me. Like right now with you."

She tilted her head against his arm, which rested on the back of the couch. "It's safe to talk to me. I'm glad you've been so open with me."

He inhaled and closed his eyes, nodding. "That's a validation I can embrace. Thanks, Cassandra. For listening."

"Anytime." She snuggled up closer to him and

spread her arm across his chest, hugging him. "This is nice. I could do this every night."

"Same. But. I need to know something. Maybe a few things."

"Like what?"

"Do you have a boyfriend?"

She squeezed him. "Do you think I'd be hugging you like this if I did?"

"Right. Also, *would* you like a boyfriend? I mean, a guy you could hang around with, date, spend time with—"

She kissed him to stop him in his struggle to find the right words. And because she wasn't sure how to answer that question. *Did* she want to be his girlfriend? Well, yes, part of her jumped for joy over the label. But another part tugged her back and waggled its finger.

You don't have time for this! Where is that ornament? Why aren't you thinking about your mom right now? And really, he's only here for the season!

Outside the patio doors a flash of brilliant sparks caught their attention and they broke the kiss.

"Sparklers," Cassandra said with growing excitement. "Dad must have brought out the party fireworks. And is that…" They both listened and the sound of a guitar and people singing rose.

"It's our guest musician! Let's go listen." She tossed him the blanket and he grabbed it.

"We could do that or...we could make out some more." He glanced toward her bedroom.

Cassandra bit her lower lip. Yes, that did feel like the next step. The most handsome boy in the school had asked her to be his girlfriend. And there hadn't been a crowd to whisper and gossip and make it wrong. She should take that win. But something wouldn't allow her to rush into What Came Next. While her body craved Rayce, her mind pulled on the brakes.

Rayce nodded. "Music and fireworks, it is." He tossed the blanket over his shoulder and offered his hand. "My stupid heart is thankful for your common sense."

"Who's to say my heart isn't as stupid? I may regret not snuggling with you in a big cozy bed tonight."

"You won't." He opened the door and gestured she lead the way out.

"How do you know?"

"I don't. But I do know that the offer will come again. You can't get rid of me that easily, Snow Princess."

"I wouldn't want to."

They clasped hands, and this time sharing a blanket, they watched the impromptu concert dazzled with sparklers.

CHAPTER THIRTEEN

THE NEXT AFTERNOON the white cat mewled, dodged Rayce's grasp and scampered across the snow-frosted patio stones. He raced after it but turned right into Brad Daniels. The man held an armload of cut wood. Despite his salt-and-pepper hair, and the fact he was at least twenty years older than Rayce, he looked fit and strong. And Rayce had learned he jogged most mornings and was on the Whistler Search and Rescue team.

"Mr. Daniels, you need some help with that?"

"I got it. Looks like you're on critter patrol."

"I want to catch that cat before it does some damage on one of the slopes."

"Good call. Did Cassandra ask you to do that?"

Rayce shrugged. "No, but I like to help out. Do things that make her happy."

Even weighed down by the wood, Brad's smile beamed. "I can see that you do. Let's talk about Cassandra."

Uh-oh, what had he stepped into? Would the man be upset he'd kissed his daughter? Well, he didn't have to confess to that. Unless Cassandra had told him. Why would she do that?

Why was he panicking?

"Cassandra," Rayce said slowly. "Yes. Your daughter. The resort manager. My, uh…boss."

"Chill, Rayce, I know you two like each other."

"You do?" Rayce winced. "Sorry?"

"What for? I haven't seen Cassie smile so much in years."

Whew! He'd won the father's approval? One major hurdle in the quest accomplished. Come to think of it, he'd achieved the quest of kissing Cassandra and altered the goal to something only his heart could describe.

"But I'm worried about her."

"Why is that, Mr. Daniels?"

Brad shifted the weight of the wood in his arms. "The lobby tree lights are still dark. She's holding on to the grief."

"Yes, we've talked about her feelings about her mom. I think Cassandra is coming around. Well, I mean, everyone grieves differently. I'd never ask her to stop…"

"Sure, and I didn't mean it like that. I just…" Brad sighed heavily. "I wonder if I moved too quickly with Faith? Does my upcoming wedding bother Cassie more than I'd expected it would? It's not like I'm replacing her mother."

"I don't think she views your engagement like

that, Mr. Daniels. She did say she was happy for you two. It's just that ornament holds a special meaning to Cassandra."

"You'll help her find it, yes? I did give her a deadline, which I believe is today. That tree needs to be lit. It's the focus. If you can help her find it, and in the process, if the two of you fall in love…" He let that sentence hang. Rayce wasn't sure he was supposed to reply so he didn't. And then Brad gave him a stern look that appeared more forced than anything. "Don't break her heart."

"Oh, I won't. Promise."

"Uh-huh." The man's assessing gaze did not preach trust.

As any father had the right, Rayce decided. And even if he were just playing with him, the implied warning had been received.

"I should get back out on the slopes. Got an appointment soon. Don't tell Cassandra about our conversation, please?"

Brad shrugged. "She's a big girl. She knows when a guy is genuine."

With that, the man strode off, arms easily supporting the heavy load, leaving Rayce behind in the cool shadows of the shed.

Did Cassandra know that he was genuine? *Was* he? What did that even mean? *Honest and kind.* The keys to a happy relationship.

His confession to her last night about having difficulty adjusting to a life lacking in fame and attention had been from the heart. Honest. She had seemed to support him. But she hadn't wanted to sleep with him. As well, she'd dodged the question about if she'd like to be his girlfriend. That had stung.

What was wrong with him? Sure, she could be taking things slow with him. Nothing wrong with that. In fact it was smart. He should follow her lead and do the same. Ignore the prodding thoughts that insisted he would never earn the nod of approval from her. Could he ever get beyond that need for validation and start to trust his own heart?

Because he'd never win the girl if he didn't get right with himself first.

The Grammy-winning musician staying at the resort had returned to the fireplace for another impromptu concert. He'd been doing so every day at random times. Two dozen guests, including Mr. and Mrs. Thorson, had gathered, hot chocolates and mixed drinks in hand, roasting marshmallows, tossing snowballs in the background.

Lured by the singer's raspy baritone, Cassandra had donned a cap and mittens and a plush comfy sweater that hung to mid-thigh to head out and enjoy the music. Thanks to their elite guest list, pleasant surprises like this happened on occasion.

The crowd was respectful, and surprisingly she only saw a few phones recording. She nodded to the security guard posted by the door and he got the hint. The resort respected everyone's wishes for privacy; they should do the same for others. When all phones were tucked away, her shoulders relaxed. Joining in on the chorus of a famous song that everyone knew, the makeshift audience raised their arms and swayed amidst the magical glow of snow-covered pine trees.

The next song, a romantic tune, lured some to dance with their partners before the massive stone fireplace.

"Would you like to dance?"

Cassandra spun to find Rayce standing behind her. His smile grasped her by the heart and squeezed. And his beautiful blue eyes made her sigh. *Caught*. And so happy for it. She nodded and as she hugged against his reassuring warmth they began to sway.

"I love this song," she said.

"Yeah, it's sappy, but the girls like it."

"Yes—" she tilted her head onto his shoulder "—we do."

With a slow twirl, they caught the Thorsons' attention. Mr. Thorson put out his fist and Rayce met him with a fist bump. The elderly couple smiled warmly and focused back on their dancing.

"Love that couple," Rayce muttered as he slid both palms across Cassandra's back and his body heat melted through her sweater. She swayed in the arms of a sure warrior. Every part of him was hard and strong, yet lean and agile. His sinuous strength made her feel protected, yet small inside his secure embrace. Like a bird protected from the wind. Closing her eyes, she succumbed to the moment.

In Rayce's arms nothing else mattered. Not the everyday troubles and astute commitment to detail required of her job. Not even that evasive ornament. And thinking that made her cling to him tightly. She didn't want this to end. He was kind, funny, and whatever was happening between them...mustn't stop. *Did* she want to be his girlfriend? At any other time she would have answered with an eager *yes*.

Why was it so difficult to step beyond her self-imposed boundaries? Were they even legitimate boundaries, or were they just silly fences erected to keep the grief inside?

Whoa. Now that was an interesting way to think about it. Was she keeping the grief in for a reason? What was it she didn't want to face?

"Song's over," he whispered as they continued to sway.

Beside them Mr. and Mrs. Thorson also still swayed to a slower tune.

The crowd sang along to a catchier tune now. Cassandra slid her hand into Rayce's. "Want to slip around the hedge?"

"Sure. Lights check?"

"No." *Move beyond that fence and kick down a few slats, Cassandra.* "Just a romantic nook."

"I am in."

Around the end of the snow-frosted hedgerow, they found a cove with a bench but they didn't sit on the padded cushion. Instead, they stood, hand in hand, in another slow dancing sway. The singer's melody echoed up and over the hedge. Christmas lights from the distant lake walk blinked in a colorful background. If Cassandra saw fairy dust fluttering in the air right now, it would feel perfectly normal.

Rayce spun her under his arm and danced her a few steps. "I like dancing with you," he said. "I don't think I've danced since high school." He got a funny look on his face, realizing something. "With you. That was my last dance."

"Really? And I ran away from you like a—"

"Like a princess who needed to beat the clock. I get it now that you've explained. But we're all alone again. And I kind of get the feeling you like my kisses?"

"Where's your mistletoe?"

He patted his coat pocket and then the back pockets of his jeans. "Darn it."

"Don't worry." She slid a hand up along his stubbled cheek. "I'll issue you a rain check on the mistletoe."

A kiss in the middle of fairyland. A dance in the arms of a man she was beginning to realize held a certain soul bond to her own. They shared so much emotionally.

"Cassandra, getting to know you has been amazing. And I think about you all the time. It feels weird to say, because it sounds so juvenile, but I like you. A lot."

"Like a lot?" She laughed. "Same."

"Really?" He bobbled the yarn pompom on the top of her white cap. "Well, what do you know. The snow princess likes me."

With a pump of his fists and a shout to the sky, he gave a hoot like the one he always shouted at the end of a winning race.

Cassandra glanced nervously toward the hedge. A crowd of guests stood just on the other side.

"Don't do that." He turned her head to face him.

"Do what?"

"Worry what others think. You're allowed to kiss a man around other people. It's not salacious. It's kind of sweet. We're not high school-ers anymore. The mean girls aren't going to whisper about you and the jock isn't going to tell all his friends he made out with you."

"I...wasn't worried about that in high school, but now I wonder if I should have been. Seriously? You would have kissed and told?"

"No, Cassandra, I mean, we're grown-ups now. We can do what we want when we want. Or is it that you don't want anyone to know you like me? Oh, that's it."

"No, it's not."

"It's an employee thing, then, right?"

"No, Rayce, I already explained—" She decided kissing him was the easiest way to end what had no strength as a viable argument. "It's just uptight me. I need to loosen up."

"I've noticed that," he said calmly, not accusingly. His eyes danced with hers. So easy to fall under his spell. Save for the one thing tugging her off course.

"Yes, well, everything surrounding me this time of year makes it hard to relax and...accept."

He took her hand, tugged off the mitten and kissed her rapidly cooling skin. "You want things perfect for your mom. I get that. But can you manage a few moments here and there for the guy who thinks you're the greatest thing since the giant slalom?"

That race had been his masterpiece. He'd never gotten the opportunity to show that to the world in the Olympics.

"I want to."

"But…?"

"But nothing." She released her breath with a nod. "Right. I'm a big girl. I've got this. And I need to stay in the moment. Right now I am standing before the sexiest, kindest, goofiest man I know, and I don't want him to think I'm not interested."

Another kiss ended what might have become an endless pep talk.

Rayce whispered aside her ear, "Let me walk you back to your room."

She hooked her arm with his. "Gladly."

Once inside Cassandra's dark apartment, they swayed before the balcony doors. The outdoor lights beamed a romantic glow across the living room.

Rayce nuzzled his nose into her hair that smelled like snowflakes, tasted sweet, with a tinge of memories. Everything about her was soft. Even her heart. Because he knew if they detoured toward the topic of that ornament, the mood would flip and he'd be spending the night in his cabin.

That wasn't going to happen. It couldn't. The

moment felt right. And when she looked up into his eyes and smiled, then began unbuttoning his shirt, he leaned in to kiss her behind the ear and down her neck. Her soft sigh turned into a wanting moan.

"Stay," she whispered. "Please?"

Rayce nodded. "Wasn't planning on leaving."

CHAPTER FOURTEEN

STARTLED AWAKE, Rayce tapped the off button on his watch alarm, and turned on the bed. Cassandra slept still, tucked between the cozy white flannel sheets. Beautiful, peaceful, gorgeous, sexy Cassandra.

Wow. That had been some sex. He really should snuggle up and—nope. He had a 7:00 a.m. appointment with a guest out on the slopes. Which was twenty minutes from now.

Swearing under his breath, he carefully slid from the bed and gathered his clothes, dressing as he made his way across the room. The curtains were pulled but subdued morning light permeated a crack between them and glowed across the bed. It dashed a line across Cassandra's pale hair.

Did he really have to leave her looking like a sleeping beauty? He'd love to wake her with a kiss and glide right back into making love. He'd be a fool to do anything but.

And yet she was so peaceful. For as hard as

she worked, and all the stress she'd been dealing with regarding her mom, she probably needed the sleep. As well, if he wanted to keep this job, he'd best make his way directly to the slope. He'd detour through the dining room on the way out. Anita would have waffles or pancakes and some form of protein to fuel his day.

Pulling on his shirt and buttoning his jeans, he stepped into his shoes at the door and wondered if he should leave her a note. Sneaking out felt a little…sneaky.

Then…he had a better idea.

Waking in the bed by herself was normal for Cassandra. But it shouldn't have been so this morning. Rayce had snuck out without even saying goodbye. Before allowing anxiety to even stir, she had the common sense to glance outside and spotted his neon green winter gear on a slope. He must have had a guest appointment this morning.

After a long hot shower she wrapped a robe about her body and wandered to the desk to check her schedule for the day. Usual rounds and then some thank-you notes, along with gifts to their best guests. This time of year her mom had always sent out gift baskets to a list of dozens. Champagne, chocolates and pastries made by local artisans, and a set of Cobalt Lake Resort branded cozy slippers and a winter scarf along with a handwritten note.

Assembling everything and writing the notes would keep her busy all day.

A knock at the door was followed by Anita slipping in. "Good morning!"

"Thanks, Anita. How's your day so far?"

"Busy. No time to chat."

"Do you have the chocolates boxed for the thank-you gifts?"

"I do. I'll have Zac bring them up right away."

"Thanks!"

The door closed and Cassandra put her feet up on a padded stool and leaned back in her chair. A relaxed coziness had encompassed her since she'd slid out of bed. Like she hadn't a care in the world. There was no rush to get things done. No one required her approval or answers to resort-related questions. She could simply exist.

Then she realized this feeling was that of having been well-pleasured last night. Had it been that long since she'd had an utterly soul-shuddering orgasm? The lingering dopamine was truly the best kind of anxiety medication. Seriously, she needed to take care of her physical needs more often. With Rayce.

She wondered if he felt the same? Had it been difficult for him to leave her this morning? Or had he snuck out, relieved to have escaped the awkward "morning after" chat?

She hoped it was the former. But there was something about Rayce that he kept closed off. Not that she expected him to reveal all and be super open—everyone had their secrets—but… she was putting too much measure on their having slept together. Maybe?

Most definitely. Let it be fun and exciting, she told herself. Just like the Christmas season should be.

With a sigh she tugged up the thick robe and closed her eyes to imagine Rayce's hands gliding over her body. His kisses tasting her. Their heat melding in a hot and heavy lovemaking session. She wanted more than lighthearted fun and excitement.

But what did that mean? Did she desire a relationship with the man she hadn't known very long but whom she had dreamed about on occasion over the last decade? A man who was only here until spring?

She had no grand designs on her future regarding relationships, but it was a "back of the mind" goal to someday have a husband, some kids and a house at the base of a mountain. Never far from the resort. This place was truly her life.

But was it her home?

That odd question startled Cassandra. Of

course, the resort was her home. Well. It was her workplace. The apartment was—no, it wasn't a home, exactly. It was where she landed after work, and continued to work, and...

"I don't really have a home," she whispered. Much like Rayce. The realization sunk heavily in her chest. "I want one." But that would involve...

Moving forward. Leaving behind the things she'd become accustomed to calling a home. Opening her heart to more than work. Letting go of some of the control. Sharing herself with another person in every way.

The thought that her mother would never be able to watch her walk down the aisle saddened her. And that switch to memory reminded she did still have a mission.

"Guest thank-you boxes to assemble," she said, "then one last ornament search before Dad realizes I've stretched the deadline by a day."

Turning over the cup on the tray, this time she sighed and caught her chin in hand at the sight of the little drummer boy. A second appearance? He could show up in her life all he wanted.

Rayce noticed Cassandra walking from the direction of the storage room. That ornament haunted her like—a precious lost mom. He'd allow her that need to hold a piece of memory in her hand. He hadn't anything but photos on his cell phone to remember his grandparents by, and he cherished them.

He wasn't sure if he dared talk to her now when she had clearly been looking for the ornament. She might be in a fragile state of mind. And him walking up to her and asking if she'd enjoyed last night would not exactly go over in the resort lobby and—who was she talking to now?

Cassandra greeted a man at the reception desk. Then he leaned in to *kiss her on the cheek.*

"What the heck?" Rayce murmured. That had been more than a friendly European greeting. And they were not in Europe.

Anita strolled toward Rayce with a tray of what looked like stacked egg cartons. She nodded acknowledgment. When she drew parallel, he asked, "Who's Cassandra talking to?"

The sous chef paused and glanced over a shoulder, her eyes taking in the pair at reception. Then she chuckled. "Oh, him! He comes every December to see her."

"What? Why? Who is he? He looks about our age. And he's..." He didn't want to admit it, but the guy was handsome. In "a crisp white shirt and slicked back hair" kind of businessman way.

"She used to date him. For a season? I don't recall how long."

Used to was good. But. Rayce's neck muscles tightened. A flash of seeing Rochelle kissing the American skier made him wince. The catalyst to his crash.

"Do they…still have a thing?"

"A thing?"

He shrugged. "You know."

How to explain, or simply ask the woman if Cassandra was getting it on with the tall handsome man she had just hugged?

"Not sure," Anita said. "Like you mean sex?" She winked.

He managed to nudge up his shoulders in an "I could care less" manner. "Not that it matters."

"Oh, it matters to you." She smiled as she walked away and called back cattily, "It matters!"

Yeah, it mattered. Because he didn't sleep with women just because he could. Despite the way the press had portrayed him as a rogue of the slopes, Rayce was a gentleman and he never slept with a woman unless he thought there was something between them. Like he had with him and Rochelle. And he'd thought that something existed between him and Cassandra. Really, they had established a connection that felt genuine.

He watched from behind a frosted white wreath smelling of spiced oranges as she led the man toward the back patio door. Really? She was going somewhere with him? Should he walk out there?

Introduce himself? Or play it cool and observe them from afar?

Since when did spying fall on the *cool* side of the scale? Rayce shook his head. They looked cozy. And if they'd once dated…

Shoving his hands in his pockets, he turned the opposite way. Just when he'd thought he'd gotten on a good run, found someone special, he'd crashed. That had been a fast fall.

With a sigh and a lift of his shoulders, he shook his head. "No," he muttered. "I will not fall this time."

It was late by the time Rayce completed his guest appointments and gathered the necessary accoutrements to visit Cassandra's room. The fresh flower arrangement in the café was now minus a long-stemmed red rose, but he'd been sneaky and squished two flowers together to hide the spot. He'd combed his hair instead of sliding his fingers through it a few times. And he'd shaved carefully so there were no nicks. He smelled like a cedar cabin—subtle, one spray of cologne—and he wore an ironed shirt.

Now he knocked on Cassandra's door, holding the flower behind him as he waited.

After seeing her talking to that man in the lobby, he'd initially grown angry. And defeated. The horrible memory of watching Rochelle kiss another skier had made it difficult to breathe. But then something inside him had sat up. That stupid heart of his? Yeah, it had grown smarter over the past days. And it suggested to Rayce the man he'd seen talking to Cassandra had probably been a friend, or a guest she'd known for some time. Nothing for him to lose his cool over. Not worth his anger.

But something niggled at him still. The twosome had walked outside together. And Cassandra had not tried to find him this evening. She knew his schedule. Which made him wonder if she was avoiding him. For what reason?

The door opened and Cassandra, standing in a fluffy white robe, smiled at him. "Rayce. I was hoping I'd see you again."

"Again? I do live here at the resort. Why would you think you wouldn't see me again?"

Her smile dropped. "What's up with you?"

Don't let your heart grow stupid again and ruin this. Be honest. Be kind.

"Sorry. Nothing's wrong. Well. Can I come in?" He whipped around the rose and offered it to her.

"Oh, that's beautiful." She stepped aside to allow him entry as she sniffed the flower. "Wait a minute. Where did you—"

He turned and winced just as she realized the answer to her inquiry.

Putting up a palm, she shook her head. "Doesn't matter. It's the thought that counts, right?"

"It is." Whew! He'd narrowly avoided that little tiff. "So it looks like I caught you getting ready for bed." He looked around. Low lighting in the living room. The humid scent of a recent shower lingered. "You have a busy day?"

"It was a long one. A bunch of reservation switcheroos and we've a high-profile celebrity staying in a week. I've already received a call from the local newspaper wanting the scoop. One of the most difficult parts of my job is detouring the media. How was your day?"

She wandered into the kitchen and found a vase for the rose. Rayce rubbed his jaw. How to ask about the man? Was it really necessary? He should ignore it—but his heart couldn't. He just needed to do it, get it out of his brain, and then he'd know it was nothing and that he could trust her.

"My day was great," he offered. "The Thorsons have graduated from the bunny hill to Harmony. They're going to be world-class skiers in no time. I love that couple. They've taught me a lot."

"Really? Like what?" She sat on the arm of the sofa, pulling a blanket over her legs. Undone and fresh from a shower, she looked so simple and perfect. He wanted to pull the robe from her shoulders and kiss her skin. Inhale her "flowers under snow" scent.

Concentrate, man!

"Uh…right. The Thorsons have shown me that I can be proud of some things. I taught them how to ski. That is an accomplishment."

"Of course it is. You have many things to be proud of, Rayce."

"I like that you're on Team Ryan, but…" He exhaled. He probably didn't have to bring it up.

Just move on. It was nothing.

"But?"

He scrubbed the back of his head, then blurted out, "I saw you talking to a guy at reception earlier. He…gave you a kiss."

"A guy? Kissed me? Oh! You mean Clint?"

Clint? Ugh.

"It wasn't a *kiss*-kiss," she said lightly, unaware of his inner emotional torment. "Clint is just a friend. Oh, wait. Did you and your stupid heart think otherwise?"

He winced.

"Oh, Rayce."

"Hey, you can do whatever you want."

"Really?"

He shrugged. "Not like we're dating."

"We're not?"

What was she getting at? He *wanted* them to be dating. They'd made love, for heaven's sake! But…Clint?

"Rayce, I don't sleep with any man who crosses my threshold."

"Well, I just—"

"Is that what you think of me?"

Her outrage stung, and he checked his cocky attitude. "Of course not. Cassandra, I thought…"

But his heart held a rein on his tongue, not allowing him to state what he really wanted. Because this felt like a race he'd forever fail.

She stepped up to him. Her soft blue eyes melted him like a snowman puddled before a bonfire. Rayce recalled the slip of her silken hair over his skin last night. Too luxurious. A treat he hadn't deserved. And yet the woman made him feel less broken.

"You thought?" Testingly she repeated his last words. "You thought what? That we *are* dating?"

He nodded subtly.

"So did I!" she declared with a gesture of her hands. "I never sleep with a guy unless there's something there. Something I want and like and well—no. I'm not going to beg for your forgiveness, Rayce. Especially since there's nothing to forgive. Clint and I did date. Years ago. But Clint stays at Cobalt Lake Resort every December. I ran into him at reception and he told me about his engagement. From there I walked with him for a while as we caught up on the past year. So if you need to do the he-man affronted act after learning that, then I guess you're not the man I thought you—"

Hearing that information snapped his self-imposed reins. Rayce slid his hands through her lush hair and pulled her in for a kiss. An urgent kiss that he'd been holding back since he'd opened the door to see her standing there like a lost snow princess desperately in need of a warming hug. She shivered in his embrace. That wasn't from the cold. Because the same shiver shuddered through his system and warmed him from the inside out. Kissing Cassandra never felt wrong. Had he been angry with her? Thought she'd gone behind his back with another man?

"I'm sorry," he said and bowed his forehead against hers. "It's my stupid heart."

"Stop calling it stupid, Rayce. I can understand how you might have taken seeing Clint give me a kiss on the cheek. But you're the only man I'm interested in. We shared an amazing night last night. I wanted to find you all day but was so busy and I know you worked late."

He kissed her again. "My he-man gene reared its ugly head. I'm a guy, Cassandra. I don't like seeing my girl with another man."

"Your girl?"

He shrugged. "I'd like that, but…"

"But?"

"It's this." He took her hand and placed it over

his heart. "My luck with women tends toward the life-destroying."

"Rayce, what are you talking about?"

Could he be completely honest with her? It would allow her to know exactly where she stood with him. And why he'd reacted so strongly to seeing her with Clint. If he didn't confess now, he may lose her. And this wasn't a race he was willing to forfeit.

"Sit with me."

She snuggled up beside him on the couch. The moment was too intimate to destroy with his truth, but it was now or never. He'd come here to make sure he did not stew in anger over something he'd been mistaken about. He owed her his truth.

"The reason I keep calling my heart stupid?"

He peered into her beautiful gaze and his anxiety lessened.

Safe here with her.

Never had he felt so sure of that.

"It's because it doesn't know how to judge a good thing from the bad. The last girl I dated resulted in my crashing at the Olympics."

She twisted in his embrace to stare up at him and did not assault him with numerous questions, and that made a difference. He needed to exhale and summon downright bravery for the next part. Would the truth change the way she thought of him? Would it send him crashing again, only this time metaphorically, but in an even more painful manner? The idea of another rejection after he'd experienced so much letdown following the accident tensed his muscles.

When her fingers threaded with his, Rayce closed his eyes and focused on the warmth of her skin. Cassandra helped him to think forward instead of wallowing in the past. She would never do anything to hurt a person or manipulate them in any manner.

"I was secretly dating a girl on the Canadian team," he started. "Rochelle. Thing is, Coach had a rule about us dating while on tour. He said dating a team member was bad news. He even encouraged us not to date at all because we're always training and competing. Intimacy before a big race? It doesn't work for some people. It's never affected me. Until I let my stupid heart into the act."

The squeeze of her fingers silently reassured him in a way he couldn't believe he deserved. When had a woman ever sat quietly with him and listened to him spill open his heart? Never.

Because he'd not trusted someone until now.

"It had only been a few weeks of us sneaking around behind everyone's backs, meeting in dark freezing start houses, slipping into a bathroom at restaurants. I really liked her, thought it was more than sneaky stolen moments behind Coach's back. My heart thought she loved me. And I thought I loved her. Maybe I did."

Tilting his head against the couch, he then shook it, utterly amazed that he'd allowed himself to soften like that. Race, crash, recover, repeat could be construed as date, crash, recover, repeat. He'd been given a hard lesson, that was sure.

"On the night before the giant slalom at the Olympics, she broke it off with me."

"Seriously? How awful!"

"Yeah, well. In hindsight we were both in it for the sex."

"But what about your stupid heart?"

"My stupid heart thought something was real when it wasn't."

"Love is love, Rayce. It comes in all forms. You probably were in love with her."

"Maybe." Yes, at the time he had thought he was in love. Yet dismissing that feeling was the only way to set it aside and turn his back on it. "But that wasn't the most devastating part. The next day, as I made my way to the start house for the big race, I saw her standing on the sidelines. I winked at her, because even though it was over..." He sighed. "Stupid heart."

Cassandra slid her hand across his chest and

hugged him closer. She was so sensitive to his need for a listening ear!

"Anyway," he continued, "when she saw me, she turned and kissed the guy standing next to her. He was on the American team and my biggest rival. And it wasn't a short peck. It was—" He swore quietly. "It ripped at me. It shouldn't have, but it did. I didn't want to believe she did it on purpose to mess with my race. I mean, we were on the same team. My loss was her loss! But it happened."

"So when you went down the slope...?"

"I thought my head was in the game, but seeing that kiss messed with my focus. I couldn't maintain my balance when my right ski hit an ice ridge on the seventh gate. I can't even recall how I went from upright on two skis, to lying on my back, sprawled, staring up at the sky. And as I lay there in a mangled mess, in pain, all I could think was, you did it to yourself, buddy. You shouldn't have been fooling around. Coach Chuck warned you. Your stupid heart."

"Oh, Rayce, I'm so sorry. I can't believe... Have you talked to her since?"

"She stopped into the hospital—" he swiped a hand over his face "—with the American skier. She acted like that sideline kiss never happened and we had always been just friends. It was another sound blow to my heart. I know I should have been stronger, but I'd never had anyone toy with my heart like that before."

"I can't imagine how that must have felt."

"Worse than the pain of the accident."

"Sorry, Rayce." She rested her head against his shoulder. "Thank you for telling me that."

They clasped hands over his heart. That she wasn't admonishing him for his stupidity and loss of focus over something so ridiculous as seeing a woman kiss a man meant the world. No judgment. Just a quiet acceptance.

"Yeah, well, it wounded me. Beyond the scars and surgeries and all the physical therapy. It hit me here." He tapped his heart. "The pain from the scarring puts an unwanted fear in my bones every time I hit the slopes, but I think that betrayal twisted its way into my soul. I don't want to crash again because some woman touched my heart and then crushed it. So when I saw you talking with Clint…"

"I understand. But I hope you realize it's not the same thing. Clint is engaged. The two of us are old news. I would never do anything to make you crash, Rayce. Promise."

"That sounds…like something my heart needs to hear."

"But you don't believe me?"

Yes, he did. Most of him did, anyway. One thumping section of his heart still held back.

"Maybe I need to put on the brakes and take it a little slower. Make sure my heart…"

"Your heart isn't stupid. It's real and wanting, and—I can imagine how you must crave love and attention after all you've been through in your life."

She rested her chin on his shoulder and placed a palm over his chest. Right over his thundering heart. He'd never told anyone about seeing Rochelle kiss the American skier. Never wanted anyone to know it had been his stupid romantic heart that had caused him to crash and literally alter his life forever.

Did she really understand that he had to be careful with his heart now? It had been him who had pursued her. Another quest, like a race, he'd had to complete. Chasing after something that might have given him the love he desired? Was that it? *Did* he crave love and attention? That sounded so needy. And yet he felt good when with Cassandra. Less broken. He didn't know if she loved him. But he did know it felt great to be with her. To receive her attention.

How could that be a bad thing?

"I care about you, Rayce," she said quietly. "And I never would have slept with you last night if you didn't matter to me. So you know, I consider us a pair."

"Yeah?"

"And if you don't, then we're going to have a different discussion."

"I like being a pair with you. But…" There was another elephant in the room that he couldn't be sure wouldn't trample them both. "Is *your* heart really in this?"

"What do you mean?"

"I know what it's like to lose someone, Cassandra. Two someones. Can your heart be in this pair with the distraction of grief?"

"You don't think I can care about you while also grieving my mother?"

"I'm sure you can. It's just, I don't want to step into a situation where you're trying to work something out, and then make it more difficult by introducing romance and love and all that jazz."

"All that jazz sounds kind of nice. But you're right. I am having a hard time of it." Twisting to settle her side against his, the back of her head nestled against his shoulder. "I know it's not about the ornament. But my heart is convinced it is. I've thought about making a special and private place in my heart for my mom, but it feels like shoving her away and reducing that heart space for her. It doesn't feel right. What am I doing wrong?"

"You're not doing a single wrong thing." He kissed the top of her head. "Everyone grieves differently, Cassandra. I can't tell you how to do it. But I can say that for myself, it was a process. I mourned. I screamed. I kicked things. I had the distraction of training to not let me get mired in falling apart after losing the two most important people in my life. But I also believe they would have been upset to watch me fall apart. The way Gramps and Grams died was an accident. But me holding a candle for them without seeing the world around me wasn't right.

"I thought about it one night. What if my mourning for them was somehow keeping them tied to the earthly realm? What if every thought I had about them anchored them to me and kept them from moving onward, going to Heaven or a new life? The best thing I could do was release them. Not from my heart. But from the part of me that needed to hold tight."

"That sounds—" she swallowed "—difficult."

"It's an adjustment. I still thought about them before every race. Gave them a nod. Gramps, who was an armchair astronomer, believed we are all stardust. I like to think the two of them are out there…stars in the sky."

"So you think I need to release my mom's memory to move onward?"

"No, you should always hold on to the memories. Don't be afraid to live your life. Don't you think that's what your mom would want for you?"

"Yes. She'd be angry to see me moping about some silly ornament."

"It isn't silly. It's something very personal to you. But you remember it, don't you?"

She curled up against his side. "I remember getting the glue all over my fingers and being so worried it wouldn't be perfect. But it was. Mom hugged me for the longest time after I gave it to her."

"That's an awesome memory. One you'll always have, even without the ornament. Just give it a think, Cassandra. I'll be here for you. But I don't want to get in the way of you finding what works for you and the memory of your mom."

"That's the kindest thing anyone has ever said to me," she said with a sniffle. "At the funeral everyone was like, *let me know what you need*. Well. I'm not going to reach out to anyone and say help me or hold me. That feels too scary, and needy. I wanted them to just do it for me without being asked. It's so weird when someone dies."

"Same happened to me. I wanted someone to hug me and make me dinner and clean my house."

"What?"

He shrugged. "My place was a mess after the funeral. I'd been out of town for months beforehand. And I wasn't in the headspace to do any cleaning. It's the little things that matter."

"That's so right. I laid in bed for days following the funeral. Then Anita knocked on the door and set a tray with hot chocolate on it by the bed, kissed my forehead and said she'd see me tomorrow morning to start the rounds my mom usually did. And you know? I did see her the next morning."

"Anita's a good one."

"She and Mom were close. I—gosh, I should talk to her about Mom someday. She's never said much. And I haven't known how to talk to anyone about it other than my dad."

"It might be a meaningful conversation for both of you. Anita knows things. She's a keeper."

"You have a weird relationship with her."

Rayce chuckled. "I think I've charmed her."

"That's one of your talents." She hugged him. "Will you stay with me tonight? No making love, just…us?"

"Definitely."

CHAPTER FIFTEEN

SLIPPING OUT OF BED, Cassandra tiptoed into the kitchen and pulled out a pitcher of orange juice. They'd slept in their clothes, snuggling until they'd fallen asleep. That quiet embrace had seemed even more intimate than sex now that she thought about it. Trust had grown between them.

With no breakfast food in the fridge, she decided that making an order with the chef would be best. Peeking into the bedroom, she saw Rayce was awake. "You hungry?"

"Always." He rolled onto his back, stretched out his legs and wiggled his feet covered with thick wooly socks. "What are you making?"

"Oh, dear one, you need to know I've become very reliant on the chef since I made the resort my permanent home. I can call Anita and put in an order for us."

"Sounds like a plan…" He glanced at his watch and winced. "Shoot. It's quarter to nine."

Had they really slept that late? She'd been so

utterly comfortable lying beside him, like being with him was the only place she belonged. "Lesson?"

"In fifteen minutes. I'm sorry, I don't have time for food." Swearing, he tumbled out of bed. A few swipes of his fingers through his hair worked his coiffure into place.

Were they destined to forever see him fleeing the scene following any night of shared intimacy? It was funny to consider.

"I can't have the boss knowing I was late because I was sleeping with his daughter. Even if it was just sleeping."

"You most certainly cannot. I'll…"

"What's so funny? You've got a laugh just waiting to escape."

She took in his unruly hair and noticed the crinkled skin on his cheek from sleeping on that side. So cute. Utterly cuddly. And about the sweetest guy she'd ever known. "You're adorable. I'll have breakfast sent out to the slopes. Something you can eat on the go."

"Thanks." Rayce grabbed his jacket and threaded in an arm. He stalked over to her with one boot on and bent to kiss her. "I gotta go! The Thorsons need me!"

As he rushed to the door, Cassandra called out, "Your grandparents would be proud of you, Rayce!"

He paused with the door open, still shoving one foot into his boot. "That's the nicest thing anyone has ever said to me."

"I wasn't trying to be nice. I just know they would be. You've got something, Rayce. People are comfortable around you. They trust you. And you're a world-class skier. Put them all together and you make a great teacher."

"Never would have thought I'd want to do what I'm doing now. But I do enjoy it. I only signed on for the season, though. Your dad just wanted to try me out."

"Would you stay longer if he asked?" And if her heart insisted?

"There is a lot here at Cobalt Lake Resort to want to stay for." If he used that wink one more time, she may have to drag him between the sheets and strip him bare. "Meet me later for some real food?"

"Sure. When do you have a break?"

"Not until four."

"Meet me back here then."

"It's a date!"

The delivery truck had picked up the thank-you gifts, all boxed up and addressed to guests. Cassandra had made up extra boxes, one for each of the resort employees. She'd handed Kathy at reception a box and the woman had eagerly dug into it, swooning over the chocolate truffles and thanking her with a high five.

After a long day, Cassandra recalled her conversation with Rayce as he'd scrambled out the door this morning. They had a dinner date this evening. She called in an order to the kitchen and was on her way to pick it up when she overheard a conversation in the lobby between what looked like an eight-year-old girl and her mother.

"Mommy, can I turn on the lights and make the tree pretty?"

"No, dear, they probably only turn them on at night."

"But it's already dark outside!"

"I know." The mother cast a glance around the lobby. It was obvious she wanted to make her daughter happy and that child's frown was something Cynthia Daniels would have never allowed to slip past her quality control.

A heavy lump rose in Cassandra's throat. She was denying a little girl a simple Christmas joy because of her adamant refusal to do one thing. That ornament may never be found. It could have gotten crushed or broken. Perhaps last year, when the decorations were packed away by staff, someone had decided it was too damaged and tossed it.

Or it was simply missing. And she needed to

come to terms with that. She'd already pushed her father's deadline beyond the past due date.

You can do this, she coached herself inwardly.

Rayce kept a place in his heart for his grandparents. Time to arrange that place in her heart specifically for her mom. A place that would allow her room for others—like a sexy ski instructor—and to move forward.

With a heavy inhale, Cassandra drew up all her bravery and walked over to the pair. "Did I hear you wonder about the lights?"

"Why don't you turn them on?"

"Uh…"

Never lie to a child.

Slipping over to the present at the back of the tree where the controls were kept safely out of the hands of curious guests, Cassandra plucked out the remote. Her mom had always let her do the honors after the tree was decorated. And she'd pronounce "Marvelous!" as Cassandra would step back and display the glowing tree with a sweep of her hands.

"I was just going to turn it on."

I love you, Mom. This is for you.

She handed the girl the remote. "You can do the honors if you'd like to. Maybe your mom will take a picture of you doing it?"

The girl nodded eagerly and cast a glimmering gaze toward her mom, who was already lining up the shot with her phone. Cassandra slipped to the side and crossed her fingers behind her back. An immense welling of emotion flooded her system. The picture that she'd pasted into the ornament had been of her laughing in her mom's arms. A precious moment forever preserved. They'd shared so many of those moments. And she remembered them all.

Out of the corner of her eye, she noticed her dad standing near the reception desk. His nod and thumbs-up to her spoke volumes. It sent her courage and approval at the same time.

With that reassurance…she relaxed. This little girl would have many memories of her mother as well. Together they may even preserve one of them in a special way, as Cassandra had.

As the Christmas lights blinked on to the cheers of the girl, Cassandra's heart opened a little wider and she embraced the moment with an accepting nod. That special place in her heart beamed.

"Thank you," she whispered, though the girl couldn't hear her through her elated cheers.

Feeling as though she'd received an approving hug from her mom, Cassandra accepted the remote back and clutched it to her chest, watching as the mother and girl took a few more shots before the beautifully lit tree. Behind, at the reception desk, her dad gave a hoot and the few guests loitering in the lobby paused to take it in.

It wasn't perfect. The ornament was still missing. But it was close enough. And maybe this time, Cassandra decided, close enough would do. Because the memory of her mom flushed her system and made her stand tall and smile. All was well.

Mostly. Maybe?

No, she had to accept this. She *could* accept this.

Meeting her dad halfway across the lobby, they collided in a long and generous hug. He kissed the top of her head and then brushed the hair from her face. "I'm proud of you, Cassie."

She nodded, the burgeoning tears making it difficult to speak.

"She lives in our hearts."

Yes, she did.

At that moment, Rayce strolled into the lobby, spied the lit tree and his eyes met hers. She shrugged. He smiled and tilted his head in a gesture that suggested she join him.

Giving her dad's hand a squeeze, she thanked him in a whisper as she kissed his cheek. "Thanks for always being there for me." They bumped fists and he wandered over to talk to the mother and her daughter while Cassandra met Rayce beside the hot chocolate dispenser.

"You just turned those on?" he asked as she joined him. "Did you find the ornament?"

"No."

He kissed the back of her hand, then held it against his cheek for a moment. "It's a good thing, Snow Princess. The tree is beautiful. Are you going to be all right?"

He understood the struggle of emotion she currently battled and knowing that settled her rising anxiety.

"Yes, I think I am. I made a place here." She tapped her chest over her heart. "For her. And I couldn't deprive the guests of such an iconic Christmas sight any longer. But that doesn't mean I'll give up my search."

"Is that where you're headed right now? On the search?"

"Actually, we had a date, didn't we? I was going to pick up our dinner and head to your cabin."

"Sounds perfect. How about after we've eaten, we drive into town and catch a movie? Like a real date?"

The hopeful tone in his voice made her smile. They hadn't gone on an official date outside of the resort.

"Sounds like the perfect way to spend an evening," she said.

His smile beamed so brightly that it extinguished any remaining anxiety she'd had about lighting the Christmas tree. With a wave to her dad, she left the lobby holding Rayce's hand.

After the movie the twosome strolled a sidewalk in Whistler Village. Christmas decorations adorned the streetlights, storefronts and even the trash receptacles, and enhanced the festive atmosphere. Rayce had spied a cozy café on the way in and wanted to stop for something sweet following the buttery theater popcorn. He'd let Cassandra pick the movie and it had been, as she'd called it, a rom-com.

"That was a cute movie," she said, clasping his hand.

"It was...too easy," he decided. "I don't think life is like that. It's more messy. Hearts and emotions can change on a dime."

"Are you talking about the movie right now? Because it sounds to me like you've switched to real life and you're not entirely convinced that what we're doing here is going to work."

"Sorry, I guess I zoned out after the hero offered to make cookies to help her win the competition." He sighed and lifted her hand to kiss it, even though she wore a glove. "Yeah, real life, eh? I want it to be like in the movies. Believe me, I've thought ahead. Like years ahead."

"And what do those future thoughts involve?"

"I think about how I'd like to have a family

and what that might look like. Having a home, for sure. I'm not going to tell you much more. Don't want to jinx it."

"A home…" Her tone went wistful for a moment, but she snapped out of it in astute Cassandra fashion. "I never think much further ahead than the day or the week's schedule."

"You're kidding me? You must have princess dreams of wearing a white dress and walking down the aisle like the chick in the movie?"

She wobbled her head. "Eh."

"But white's your color!" he said more as a prod than in disbelief.

"Okay, fine, but I've always thought a simple summer ceremony would suit me. Wearing a floral dress. Barefoot. Flowers in my hair."

Now she was just being romantic. Rayce swallowed as the image of Cassandra Daniels adorned in flowers and twirling down a grassy aisle toward him gave him some kind of hopeful quiver right…there. He caught a hand over his heart.

"What's wrong?" she asked while simultaneously pointing across the street toward the café. "All that buttered popcorn acting up?"

"Yep." And he was sticking with that story. Wouldn't feel right to confess he'd had a romantic thought about his future. A future that included his snow princess.

"Let's pick up some fancy treats to take back

with us." He tugged her ahead to a chocolate shop that displayed bonbons in the window.

"You do know the way to my heart."

Honestly? He *was* navigating some sort of passageway toward her heart. And it felt like a fresh run down a new slope: adventurous, a little risky and filled with the unknown around every slight curve. But that was exactly the kind of risk Rayce Ryan liked to take.

CHAPTER SIXTEEN

THE FOLLOWING MORNING, Rayce had lingered in Cassandra's bed. They'd kissed. Made slow and intense love. Dozed off in one another's arms. Then repeated. The man did like to practice a thing until he got it right.

He most certainly did get her right.

Bright sunlight finally coaxed them to rise and get dressed. Rayce had offered to pick up something in the café and bring it up to her, but she declined. She had morning rounds to make and he did have a client. It wasn't a rush out the door to make the appointment, though. They'd kissed all the way to the door, and when he'd gotten ten feet down the hallway, he'd spun and rushed back to give her one more long lush kiss.

Getting it right.

Now she stood before the vanity mirror after having blown out her hair and put on some makeup. She'd never felt so utterly relaxed and at the same time *desirable* in her life. It was a heady feeling. Better than Christmas morning.

The best present she had received so far this holiday season was rediscovering Rayce. Being able to share things with him. Talking about both the good and bad times. He seemed to understand her, and she understood him. They had bonded through grief. But she wanted it to go beyond that. And it did. They shared amazing chemistry between the sheets. And even when dressed and walking hand in hand or eating or enjoying life, they seemed to fit in one another's atmosphere with ease.

Finding love couldn't be so easy, could it? Because, when she thought about it, she cared about Rayce and adored every little thing about him. From his cocky grin to feeling he needed to wield the plastic mistletoe to get a kiss from her. And her heart was all in. Which meant…

Was she falling in love? So quickly?

Her dad had done as much with Faith. But he and Faith had known each other since high school.

She and Rayce had gone to school together, too, but hadn't really known one another. That hadn't stopped her from crushing on him. And, apparently, he'd had a thing for her, too. Was it only now that life had decided they should become a couple?

Why fight it? Or better, why not take it day by day and enjoy the moments? Yet the deadline for his departure lingered. If she ransomed her heart to him this winter, would she have to take it back when he left in the spring?

"Don't think like that," she admonished herself.

When he'd mentioned his plans last night, the word *home* had seemed to cling to her. More and more she really did wish for a home away from work. An escape from the place where it felt necessary to exercise control. Yet since she'd begun to loosen the reins on that control, the longing for a place to genuinely relax was real.

Dare she dream of a future with Rayce in a home they'd created together?

"Nothing wrong with dreaming," she whispered.

But the thought wasn't as convincing as it should have been. They were in a new relationship. Anything could happen. It was far too early to start picking out patterned China and silverware.

"But I can allow the fantasy," she whispered with an approving nod to her change toward a more relaxed and open future.

Dressing quickly, she combed her hair and pinned it up in a neat chignon, then headed out for her usual morning rounds.

Afterward, bundled up against the cold, she wandered over the boot-tracked trail that curled around behind the main patio and fireplace. When a *thunk* of cold snow splatted her back, she at first thought it was snow falling from the pine trees. But a distant whoop of triumph revealed to her she had been attacked. And she recognized that cocky whoop.

"Really?" Cassandra surveyed the snowy ground, spying the best patch for ammunition. When another snowball hit the back of her boot, she swung into action. Bending, she scooped up a handful of moist yet moldable snow and began to pack it. "Are you aware that I am the snowball-throwing champion of the Girl Guides of Canada?"

Rayce splayed his arms out in mock challenge. Then he tapped his chest and lifted his chin defiantly. "Take your best shot!"

He was close enough for the direct hit that she lobbed toward him. Snow dispersing at his shoulder, he took it like a man. But he quickly bent to reload. As did Cassandra.

She threw another, and another, each time landing a hit on her opponent. He missed her a few times because, now that she could see them coming, she dodged like the professional she was. They moved closer and closer, and her snowball craftsmanship grew messier until finally she held two handfuls of loose snow as Rayce ran toward her. She flung them at him, getting him in the face. His chuckles matched hers as he grabbed her about the waist and took her down in the fluffy snow.

Their kiss was cold and silly as they rolled in the snow and took turns flinging loose snow at one another. Kiss. Attack. Kiss. Pleads for mercy as snow began to sink under her scarf and icy water seeped through her sweater.

"Mercy?" Rayce defied as he hovered above her, a snowball in hand.

"Please!" she shouted.

"Then I guess we know who the new snowball champion is, eh?"

"I'll alert the Girl Guides immediately." She flapped her arms out across the snow as she lay on her back, looking upward.

Rayce flopped down next to her, and he started reshaping the snowball he had in hand.

The sky glistened with a beautiful pink tinge that floated at the tops of the snow-dusted pine trees. It had been a long time since Cassandra had lain in the snow and took things in. Lived in the moment. As well, she'd missed the utter abandon of a good snowball fight.

"Turning on the tree lights wasn't as heart-wrenching as I thought it would be," she confessed.

"I'm glad." He worked diligently at his snowball. "I bet it made your mom happy."

At the thought of her mom, smiling and laughing with happiness, a tear came to Cassandra's eye. But she wasn't going to freak about her sadness. Instead she opened that place she'd reserved in her heart and sat with it a while.

"Here." Rayce handed her the snowball.

"What's this for?"

"You."

She took the snowball; it was no longer rounded. He'd formed it into a heart.

"It's my heart," he said lightly. "I trust you'll treat it well."

She carefully held the snow heart with both gloved hands. "I'll treat it as kindly and respectfully as you've treated mine."

He rolled over to kiss her until they were laughing and wrapped in one another's arms, legs and scarves. He smelled like winter cedar and sensual heat. And he tasted like snowflakes and adventure. Amidst their make-out session, she managed to set the heart down.

Rayce looked aside to spy the snow heart. "Let's leave it there so it doesn't melt."

"Deal. Race you back to the resort?"

"If I claim an injured leg, will you give me a head start?"

"Ha!" She pulled herself up and then before dashing off, she bent over the snow heart and

drew a bigger heart around it with her finger.
"There. Now it's official."

"What's official?"

"Our hearts belong to one another."

"That's freakin' romantic."

"Yeah? Well, this isn't." She blasted him with
a kick of snow, then took off toward the resort.

He followed, his laughter the best balm to the
few slivers of grief that the thoughts of her mom
had produced. But with Rayce she realized she
could hold all those emotions, and still rise to
embrace the good times.

He didn't want to wake the sleeping beauty, so
Rayce finished a note for Cassandra and set it on
her desk. Yes, he'd developed a habit of slipping
out of her bed while she slept, but not every time.
Invigorated by a night of making love and a new-
found intimacy that included trust and honesty,
he wanted to challenge himself this morning.
And his back wasn't bothering him, so it was
now or never.

The sun wouldn't rise for another hour, but he
was eager to catch the fresh powder. He grabbed
his ski jacket and headed out.

An hour later he landed at the bottom of the
run. Exhilarating! The powder was deep and dry.
Perfect conditions for a speedy descent. And de-

spite a few painful twinges along his spine, his leg hadn't given him trouble.

But now that the sun had risen, the slope was crowded with skiers. Had he really left a warm, gorgeous Cassandra alone in bed just to catch some powder?

"Fool," he muttered.

However he'd had to prove something to himself. And now that he thought about it, the invigorating feeling that encompassed him may be pride.

"Nice." He could push his body. But as well, he'd learned that he'd hit the limit in those runs. Any faster and he would have been in agony. There were no gold medals in Rayce Ryan's future. No more cheering fans. No more endorsements or sponsorship deals. Retirement was a real thing.

Strangely he was okay with that. Because he'd found something more fulfilling.

With an accepting nod he skied over to the hot chocolate vendor. When he went to flash his employee badge for a free drink, he patted his jacket. Where was the tag?

"Sir?" the elder gentleman manning the bar prompted as Rayce patted down his clothes in search of the badge.

It must have fallen off somewhere. Probably when he'd been flying downhill. Ah, well, he had some cash in his pocket. He handed over a bill and received a steaming cup. It was far from the thick fancy stuff the resort served their guests, but the sugar worked the same, rushing through his system with a scream.

When he tossed the cup in a garbage bin and turned around, his path was blocked by three women wearing various shades of pink and purple. Snow bunnies, each with diamonds glinting at their ears and around their necks. Their sort never zipped up their jackets against the chill. How else would anyone notice their bling? They were not here for the skiing; they were here to be seen and to party.

One of them called him by name and asked him for an autograph. She offered the pink sleeve of her jacket and a black Sharpie. The others joined with their sleeves as he whisked his John Hancock down each arm. Despite the crazy good feeling of pride he was still riding, his ego would never tire of the attention. This retired Alpine racer had to take advantage of it when he could.

"We saw you fly down that slope. You're so talented, Rayce. You make it look so effortless."

The last sleeve was signed and she tipped the capped marker under his chin. Her bright pink lips curled into a seductive twist. "You want to join us in our room for something stronger than cocoa?"

"We have so many questions. If you answer them, we'll make it worth your while," she sing-songed coyly.

Rayce's eyebrows rose. The pheromones coming off them in waves were dusted with perfume and lust. He could feel it permeate his skin.

"Sorry, ladies, I don't think my girlfriend wants me answering questions."

"Girlfriend? The media reports say you haven't dated since the accident. That you were incapable of ever..." She shrugged. "You know."

Now that one stung. And it was a cruel cut at his manhood. The media had never reported any such thing!

As the trio laughed wickedly, Rayce pushed away and slid toward the track leading to the resort. They'd started out amiable enough, but when he'd refused their advances, they'd grown just plain mean.

His mood dove from the high of the early morning fresh powder run to the dredges of a bruised ego.

Cassandra found the note after Rayce had slipped from her bed without so much as a kiss good-bye. It sat next to the little drummer boy figurine and read:

Heading out to catch the fresh powder. See you later.

Seriously? He must have snuck out extremely early because the sun was only just now rising. Which meant he'd hit the slopes before they were open to the public. There was a reason the runs weren't open until the sun came up. They were dangerous; what kind of idiot went out on his own to ski in the dark?

She bit her lip and shook her head. Her mom had gone out at midnight all the time, much to her dad's protests. Such reckless abandon had cost her her life. And while Cassandra knew Rayce was a professional—it didn't matter. Mother Nature cared little about a skier's skill.

Stepping on something with her bare foot, she winced, then bent to pick it up. It was Rayce's employee badge. She turned it over. A fragment of neon green fabric stuck in the rivet clip. It had torn from his jacket.

She glanced out the patio doors. The slopes were busy; it was always a rush to get to the fresh powder in the mornings. She couldn't see the green jacket out there. Had he gone down a slope before the sun had risen and…had trouble?

A terrible darkness clenched Cassandra's throat. She didn't want to think the worst. But as she clasped the badge and the plastic edge dug into her palm, she could only think of avalanches and skiers missing their mark and careening off the slope to crash into rocks or tree trunks.

Or worse.

She swore. Just when she had been so close to accepting the loss of her mother and moving forward, now this had to happen. *If* anything had happened.

No. He was fine. Right? If an avalanche had occurred, the entire mountain would be cleared and emergency protocol would be instituted. Her dad, a member of the search and rescue team, would have alerted her. Rayce was perfectly fine. He knew what he was doing—but why would he torment her like this? He knew about her fears.

With a swallow she closed her eyes and pressed a hand against her thumping heart. Praying nothing had happened. Her heart may never recover!

Wrapping a scarf around her neck, she stepped into her boots and opened her door to find Rayce standing there with his fist up in preparation to knock.

"Rayce!" She grabbed him by the front of his jacket. "Get in here!"

"Glad to see you, too." He wandered inside and turned to give her a wink. "Is this urgent welcome because you missed me and need to strip me bare right now?"

"What?" Oh. He was talking about the fabulous sex they'd had last night. But she could not get beyond her fear and anger to soften to that pleasure. "No! You are so reckless!"

His jaw dropped open. "Reckless? Me?"

"Yes, you. Going out before the slopes opened? Were there even any patrols out there? It had to have still been dark. Did anyone see you?"

"Cassandra, are you seriously upset because I—a professional skier—wanted to take a few runs on my own? You know I know what I'm doing, right?"

"The slopes don't care if you're a professional or a newbie. You could have been hurt and no one would have known where you were."

"I left you a note. And I—" He patted his jacket and winced.

"And you left without this!" She held up the badge. "Didn't you notice it missing?"

"Not until after I'd finished my run, and then I got distracted because I was shut down by a bunch of snow bunnies with flashy bling and bad attitudes."

"Snow bunnies?" Her shoulders dropped as she exhaled. So that was what he'd been doing? "You were out there flirting while I was in here worrying about you?"

His smile grew. "You were worried about me? Does that mean you care about me?"

"Of course I care about you. But I don't like that you believe you're so expendable. I would think that the accident curbed your reckless need to endanger your life."

"I am not a reckless skier. And that accident was not due to anything but a broken heart. I told you that!" He swore. "Please don't tell anyone about that. It's humiliating. And now you're chastising me as if I'm a child!"

"Only because I would be devastated if you were injured or...or worse! I can't believe you don't understand that. After my mom—I thought we had something."

"We do. Cassandra, I wasn't thinking about your mother. I realize now that finding that badge must have freaked you out. You thought I was out there with no means to be found if... if anything had happened to me. I'm sorry. I should have—"

"Yeah? Well, my mom is never coming back because she was reckless. I'll never get to hug her again."

Something inside Cassandra closed. All the emotional work she'd put in since Rayce had arrived sluiced away. Her heart went still as the armor fitted back around it.

She lifted her chin and shook her head. The adrenaline junkie standing before gave her a bewildered look. "I can't do this. You're not the man for me, Rayce. I can't handle any more grief right now."

"Cassandra, I'm fine."

When he made a move to embrace her, she put up her hands in protest. "I need someone stable, Rayce. Someone who is willing to stick around Cobalt Lake for me. Someone who will be there for me and who won't take risks."

He sighed heavily. "Skiing is all about the risk," he muttered. "You know that."

She bowed her head and nodded. "Would you please leave?"

"Really? We have to talk about this, Cassandra. I don't want this thing we've started to end. And I'm not a loser like those ladies on the slopes implied. I can't be. But if I lose you…"

She winced. So much was unspoken in that pause. He'd lost a lot. She should be more sensitive to that. But right now, with her fractured heart, she couldn't handle another heartbreak.

She opened the door, holding it for him. "I'm sorry. I can't do this."

With a heavy sigh Rayce walked to the door but paused alongside her. She couldn't look at him. Or she'd fall into his summer sky eyes and melt.

Without a word he took a mangled piece of plastic from his jacket pocket and handed it to her. Then he left, closing the door behind him.

Cassandra clasped the mistletoe to her chest. Tears spilled down her cheeks. She didn't want him to go. But she didn't know how to ask him to return.

What was she so reluctant about? It couldn't be because of his reckless behavior. She was bigger than that. The man knew what he was doing. And no matter how safe she attempted to keep her world and those in it, she could never monitor everyone all the time. Accidents were just that—accidents.

She had been so close to allowing love into her life.

Leaning against the door, she crushed the mistletoe against her chest and closed her eyes. "I wish you were here, Mom. I need you."

CHAPTER SEVENTEEN

AFTER AN AFTERNOON class with four kids all under ten years old, Rayce helped an intern return the skis and poles to the storage shed. It had been gently snowing for an hour. Thick flakes quieted the atmosphere in a way those who weren't familiar with a snowy season could never understand. Though the slopes were still packed with skiers, it was as though sounds and conversations were muted. Nature insisted on being noticed.

With an eye to a lift on Blackcomb peak, he shook his head. His back, which had been tight and painful all day, warned him to stay grounded. A deep tissue massage and maybe even a soak in the hot tub felt necessary.

Take care of yourself, buddy. It's the right thing to do. Besides, you're retired, remember?

As well, after the argument with Cassandra this morning, he didn't need a streak of pain in his spine to warn him against taking a risky run. If he'd been feeling low after his encounter with the snow bunnies, Cassandra had shoved him even lower with her announcement that she didn't want him in her life.

As he walked slowly toward the employee cabins, he veered off behind a line of pine trees where the snow blanketed a short length of open field. He'd heard some kids out here the other night making snow angels. And despite the falling snow, he could still see impressions of an angel or two as he walked by.

The pale sky fluttered with flakes. He sighed. His two angels were up there. Somewhere.

"Are you out there?" he asked the sky. "In the stars? Do you miss me as much as I miss you?"

Talking to his grandparents helped him to forget the rough parts of life that tended to sneak up on him. Like an injured leg keeping him grounded. Or an upset woman who had told him she didn't want someone as reckless as him in her life.

The fact that Cassandra had talked about needing someone to stick around long term had been buoying. But at the time his heart sunk. Because in the same breath she'd erased *him* from that possibility.

Cassandra had made a choice. And it hadn't been him. She insisted on swimming in her grief and not allowing anyone to dive in to float alongside her. He could have done that. He thought he *had* been doing that. Talking with her. Sharing his grief with her. Being there for her.

If that badge hadn't fallen from his jacket, he'd be in Cassandra's room right now, holding her in his arms, nuzzling his nose into her hair. Being the man she wanted him to be because that was the kind of man *he* wanted to be.

Eyeing an undisturbed patch of thick snow, he turned and fell backward, arms out. He landed with an *oof* and a chuckle because he'd made an old man noise. At the very least, his leg hadn't done anything weird like twitched him headfirst into a snowbank.

Spreading out his legs and arms, he fashioned a snow angel and closed his eyes to the falling flakes. The taste of them melting on his lips reminded him of his snow princess.

Well, she wasn't his anymore, was she? She'd declared he wasn't the guy for her. That he hadn't cared enough about her to not go skiing on his own. At the time he couldn't have known the angst he was causing Cassandra. It hurt his heart to think that something he had done had upset her.

"She's very special," he said to the sky. "I thought we had something. I…don't want to be alone. I'd give it all up if I could have someone in my life. Someone to love."

He'd already lost it all, so he had nothing left to sacrifice. Was that it? He had nothing to offer someone like Cassandra Daniels. No comfy home. Not even a strong proud warrior of a man who could protect her. An injured leg did not make for a hero.

"I could fall in love with her," he confessed to the sky. "I know what love feels like. You guys made me feel safe, happy and loved. Did I ever tell you how much I appreciated what you did for me? Allowing me to go on those ski trips and funding my training. Buying all my gear. I know you weren't rich. But, Gramps, you never said no. And, Grams, you always had a hot meal and a hug for me whenever I returned home from camp or a ski event. I miss you guys!"

The wind shushed through the pines and re-directed a glittering sweep of snow across his face. If that hadn't been a message from Gramps, he didn't know what was. The old man had always been funning with him, trying to get him to laugh.

He sat up and brushed the snow from his ski pants. His cap had fallen off and he twisted to pick it up. He traced a finger over the embroi-dered Cobalt Lake Resort logo. Could this place ever be a home to him?

"I could settle here and be happy," he said to anyone who would listen.

They were listening. They always were.

"The skiing is first class. And…Cassandra." His snow princess.

He most certainly was not the best guy she

could have in her life, he thought to himself. Not smart enough, that was for sure. And too cocky, certainly. Complete opposite of her careful and neat ways. And...reckless.

But she made him believe his heart was not so stupid. Heck, the darn thing had to be smart. It had led him to Cassandra.

Should he beg her to give him another chance? That's how it worked in the movies. Grand gestures seemed to be a thing in a successful romance. Rayce shoved a hand in his pocket. He'd handed Cassandra the mistletoe in a moment of surrender, of forlorn sadness at having been given the boot. There was no easy passage back into her heart now.

But if a passage still existed, he hoped the gate wasn't locked.

"Do I dare fall in love?"

The pale sky was serene and quiet. A few snowflakes brushed his face. Kisses from his grandparents. He knew what their answer was.

Now did he have the courage to live up to their expectations? To show them that he could accept love and give love in return?

The next morning Anita dropped off a tray of hot chocolate as Cassandra was stepping out of the shower. "Have a great day!" she called.

"Wait, Anita!"

"Yes?"

Cassandra pulled on a fluffy robe and hustled out to the living room. She knew the sous chef's time was valuable, but now more than ever she was determined to honor the connection with her mom in any way possible.

"I appreciate you bringing me hot chocolate in the morning. I know you always did the same for my mom."

"Your mother and I…" Anita pressed a palm over her chest.

"You two were close," Cassandra confirmed. "She mentioned you often."

Anita nodded, not looking up. Cassandra could sense her nervousness and heard the catch in her breathing. "I cared about your mother. She was very good to me. To all of us. We chatted in the mornings. Sometimes I would take tea with her if I wasn't too busy."

"That's so nice to hear." Cassandra hadn't known that. Perhaps they'd been more than respectful coworkers, friends even. "I have wanted to speak to you about her since, well, since she passed. I want you to know that you were special to her."

"Thank you, Cassandra. She was special to me. I miss her." Now she tilted her head back and sniffed at a tear. "I know it's hard for you now. And seeing your dad with his new fiancée…"

"It took a while for me to accept Faith, but she's good for my dad. And I look forward to meeting my new step siblings. Are you okay, Anita? I mean…have you ever talked to anyone about…?" About Cynthia.

Anita shrugged and shook her head, and that action compelled Cassandra to hug her. Initially Anita resisted, but then she pulled her into a hug that drew tears from Cassandra's eyes as well.

"She is missed," Anita whispered. "But always remembered."

Cassandra stepped back from the hug and swiped a tear from her cheek. "Yes, remembered. Every day."

"But you mustn't let sadness stick to your bones," Anita said with a deep inhale as she settled her shoulders. "That's not good for anyone."

She'd never heard it put in such a manner, but yes, the grief had stuck to her very bones. And it wasn't good for her.

Anita clasped her hand and squeezed. "Thank you. I needed that hug."

"So did I."

"You are so much like Cynthia," she said. "I know she is proud of you. And you know? I think she would like that handsome Rayce Ryan a lot."

Cassandra chuckled. "I think she would, too. And if she didn't, he'd charm his way under her skin one way or another."

"He is a charmer. So, uh…"

"What is it, Anita?"

"I just think he's falling in love with you."

"You do?" Cassandra wasn't at all surprised at such a declaration. Her heart felt much the same about Rayce. But to hear it declared so simply forced her to own that feeling. "I… Well. Rayce is kind. Funny. We have fun together."

So why had she let him leave? Kicked him out, even? She'd told him she couldn't do this. That hadn't been her talking. Not rationally, anyway.

In that moment Cassandra had allowed fear to rise and overwhelm her. She hadn't been acting in accordance with her true feelings. Rayce calmed her and embraced her every quirk, mystery and even her perfectionist tendencies. Her mom would certainly approve.

Was she looking at Rayce as an option for her future? The other options being…no boyfriend, constant work, no social life, all her free time consumed with work-related tasks?

"Anita, do you think I've lost myself in this job?"

"Honestly? You do spend an awful lot of time here. Your mother had her home in Whistler Village to go to after work. Where do you go?"

"Here." Cassandra's shoulders dropped.

The words Anita didn't speak were clear: *where is your life?*

"I do dream about having a home away from work. And about having a relationship with Rayce."

"Your mother would be happy to hear that." Anita took Cassandra's hand and gave it a squeeze. "Take a chance on him. He's a great guy."

Well. Rayce did have his reckless moments. And that would never change. Also he didn't trust his own heart. She hated that he called it stupid. A person should never use that word to describe any part of themselves. The body listened to those words. And if he couldn't get beyond not trusting his heart, that could present a problem should she decide to offer up her own.

But did *she* trust her heart?

"I do want to give him a chance," she said. "Or rather, I did. We had an argument. Oh, I wish my mom were here to talk to. But…" She inhaled and let it all out through her nose. *Let it go.* "I can't thank you enough for letting me talk to you like this. It means a lot."

"Anytime, Cassandra. And don't worry. People argue. It's what we do to learn about one another, yes? And then we realize it's not worth the anger. If you care about him, tell him."

Cassandra nodded as Anita left and closed the door behind her. She did care about Rayce. And she had come down from her anger enough to realize their argument had been hasty and not at all what her heart desired.

So much had happened since Rayce Ryan had set foot in the resort. Her heart had altered in many ways. She had conceded and turned on the tree lights without finding the ornament. Because it had made others happy. And in the process, it had brought a smile to her face. It had lightened her grief to know her mother would have approved.

This was supposed to be the happiest time of the year. A wonderful life! Yet one moment her heart swelled with joy, the next it sank into sadness.

Closing her eyes, she pictured her mom. Pale blond hair and tall lithe figure. Always elegantly dressed and, though Cassandra knew Cynthia Daniels's brain always spun one hundred kilometers an hour and never slowed down, she wore a smile for others and her kindness was always genuine.

"What do you think, Mom? About Rayce? He's special. He makes me laugh. I have fun with him. I forget about work and striving for perfection when I'm with him. I think I could love him."

Silent, she waited in quiet wonder for a vocal reply she knew would never come.

Did she need a sign? She liked hearing how

Rayce thought of his grandparents as stars in the sky, always there, watching over him. Maybe her mom was up there, too. And if so…

"I have to follow my heart, with you as my guide."

With a nod she confirmed the conversation with Anita had been worthwhile. Her mom, who never took time to slow down and chat with anyone, had spent time in the mornings over tea with Anita. Another wonderful memory to store in that place in her heart designated for Cynthia Daniels.

Eyeing the tray, with the pot and upside-down teacup, her heart skipped. Would she find a surprise under the cup this morning?

Her heart sank. Probably not. She and Rayce had come to some sort of ending. Much as she regretted it. Was it too late to change things? It couldn't be. The man was good for her heart.

If she wanted Rayce, she had to fight for him.

With another determined nod, Cassandra got dressed. Sitting before the desk to check her emails before she started her rounds, she again eyed the upside-down cup. The suspense was killing her, and yet…

She shook her head and tapped at the keyboard to go through a short list of emails. The RSVPs for the employee Christmas party were pouring in. They always held the gathering a few days before Christmas Day itself, and brought in a celebrity chef and entertainment from Whistler. Secret Santa gifts were exchanged while photos were taken. No one ever missed it.

An email from Faith reminded her she had promised to go wedding dress shopping with her and her daughter after the New Year and gave her a few dates as options. The idea of gaining not one but three new family members had initially shocked her. Then she'd decided it was good for her dad. He needed the companionship, love and attention. And why not? Love did things for a person's heart.

And she was beginning to recognize that change in her own heart.

Typing a reply to Faith to say that any of the dates would work, Cassandra then absently reached for the teacup and turned it over, completely expecting the saucer beneath to be bare—

Cassandra let out a surprised chirp. Sitting on the plate was a small silver star that she knew had come from one of the wreathes in the lobby. Made of resin, it glittered when she tilted it. She recalled again how Rayce thought of his grandparents as stars in the sky.

With a tearful smile she tapped the star. "I haven't given up on you, either, Rayce."

CHAPTER EIGHTEEN

RAYCE SPIED THE white cat scampering over a snowbank and toward the equipment sheds. He took chase. Angling toward the employee cabins, he swung around a tall birch tree only to collide with Cassandra. He caught her by the forearms and steadied her from taking a fall.

"Are you okay?"

"Yes. Thanks for catching me. But what are you doing out here?"

He had not planned to literally run into her after their breakup. They'd both said terrible things. Had put their hearts out there. And it hadn't ended well. He owed her an apology. More than that, he wanted to talk until they moved beyond the argument and back into the trust and empathy they'd created.

Look at him, feeling all, well...the feelings!

"I'm on the trail of a wayward cat," he said. "You?"

"Same. I think it went that way." She pointed toward one of the vehicle sheds.

He bent to study the snow. "You are correct. Tracks!" He grabbed her hand and led her quickly across the snow. To talk now or wait until the moment was right? The moment might never be right. But what if he made the wrong move? Again!

A *crash* from inside the shed averted his attention. "Let's get that cat! I'm sure it went into the shed."

"I don't know how it could get inside. The building should be locked and…"

As they neared the shed, both were shocked to see one of the windowpanes was broken. Nearby on the ground lay a broken pine branch. Evidence that it hadn't been a purposeful break-in.

"That's a very crafty cat." Rayce inspected the tracks that leaped from the ground and landed on the windowsill to disappear inside. He peered through the broken window. "Here, kitty, kitty!"

"Let's check inside." Cassandra led him around the corner to the front door where she entered the digital code.

Inside the open-beam structure sat a fleet of the resort's vehicles. A Jeep and a four-wheeler were parked on one side, as well as some of the facility equipment. There was no need to flick on a light switch because daylight beamed through the half-dozen glass ceiling panels.

Rayce scanned around the room filled with assorted vehicles and his gaze landed on the scatter of broken glass. "You got a broom in here?"

"Don't worry about it." Cassandra inspected the glass that had fallen inside. "I'll send the groundskeeper out to clean it up and repair the window. We'll use the fallen branch in the fireplace tonight."

"You've always got everything under control. I adore that about you."

"Hmm, well, I do fall apart on occasion."

He opened his arms and gestured with his fingers. "Come here. Fall into me."

In her moment of reluctance, he watched as caution played over Cassandra's face, only to quickly wriggle into something familiar and much more welcome: trust. Cassandra plunged into his embrace and the two kissed in the dim quiet. Broken in different ways, they had learned to understand themselves through one another.

"You make the world kinder," she said to him.

"I don't know about that. We need to talk, Cassandra. I'm sorry."

"I am, too."

"Yeah? Well, hear me out." He exhaled a cloud of breath. "I'm willing to risk rejection for the prize. The crowd can boo all they like. If I feel what I'm doing is good, that's all that matters."

"What does that mean?"

"I like it here at the resort, Cassandra. I'm

going to talk to your dad about staying on through the summer."

"Rayce, that's wonderful. We'd love to have you for as long as you're willing. I know my dad would agree. But what prompted your change of heart? I thought you had intended to train…?"

"That was boasting, Cassandra. It'll never happen. And you know? I don't want that anymore. The competition and relentless training? That was the first part of my life. Retirement feels right."

"It does?"

"It does. So now? Here? It feels like a new beginning. One I want to follow to the end."

"I'm proud of you."

He studied her face, beaming at him beneath her pink pompom cap. In Cassandra's eyes he never felt like he had to prove himself. Yet hearing her say she was proud of him felt like a million sparklers had just been lit in his body. He absolutely hummed with a jittery excitement. "Really?"

"Yes. You're following your heart. A very smart heart that may make mistakes sometimes, and then other times makes some very good decisions. It's not stupid. It's real. We all get hurt, Rayce. I'm sad that you were so devastated by what you thought was your heart, but you know, maybe that was the way life intended your path to go."

"Those are profound thoughts. I'm not much for destiny and all that fate jazz. I just…" He had to go for the gold if he wanted this to work. The anticipation of the moment felt as bright as his inner sparklers. Could she see his nervous excitement? NASA space satellites must be able to see it. "There's another reason I want to stay here. It's because of you."

"Oh, Rayce, I…"

"I know what you said about me being reckless. I promise to do a badge check every hour. To never be off your radar."

"Thank you, for that reassurance. I shouldn't have gotten so upset. I know you are a professional. You can take care of yourself. It's just…"

Just what? Some of the sparklers extinguished. She couldn't reject him. Please?

"Mother Nature doesn't care how skilled or smart we are," he said. "I get it, Cassandra. And I want to stay safe. Because you matter to me. And I'd hate to know something I did caused you any worry or pain."

He kissed her. First on her cheek, then on her lips. Her lashes fluttered against his nose as he tilted up to kiss her on the forehead. Marking her indelibly. Making a claim that could only be interpreted by his heart. He took her gloved hand and placed it on his chest. She probably couldn't feel his heartbeat through his jacket, but who knew? Every piece of him felt turned up to eleven. And he had to make her understand that feeling.

"This place feels like it could be a home to me," he confessed. "That's part of what I really want."

"It can be your home."

"I don't mean a little cabin behind the resort. I mean like moving back to Whistler, becoming a member of the community. Doing…life stuff."

"Life stuff?"

"Like owning a home and car and having a family. Making a career of teaching others how to ski."

"You have big plans."

"They are small compared to what I have with you right now. The other part of what I want is… It's you, Snow Princess. Do you think we can continue this relationship? I promise I won't break your heart."

"You don't need to make any such promise. I shouldn't have yelled at you like I did." Now she pressed both her palms to his chest and considered her words before finally saying, "I've been leery, too. Trying to relax my tight control on everything, including letting go of my grief. But I had a talk with my mom today."

"You did? I talked to my grandparents earlier."

"I know you were thinking about them."

She…knew? He gave her a wondering gape.

"I got the star under my teacup." She kissed him. "You were talking to your two stars up above, weren't you?"

"I was," he said in awe of her understanding. She got him. And knowing that made him feel even better than knowing she was proud of him.

"Mom would want me to enjoy life," she said. "To put my heart out there. For someone to catch."

He kissed her hard. Deeply. And in the process transferred those shimmering sparkles he experienced to her. Clutching her to him, Rayce whispered, "Caught you."

"Don't ever let me go."

"Promise I won't."

A sudden cloud of dust fluttered down from the rafters. "That's weird."

"Kitty!" Rayce called repeatedly.

She followed his sightline as he scanned overhead along the rafters.

"I think the critter is up there—watch out!" He grabbed her about the shoulders and tugged her aside.

A falling cat snarled through the air. A box crashed three feet from where they stood, tearing cardboard and scattering the contents in a tangle of Christmas tree lights, tinsel and plastic lighting clips.

Secure in Rayce's arms, Cassandra hugged him tightly. Her rescuing hero. Who simply wanted a home. A place for his heart to be happy.

The cat *meow*ed and wandered to the scatter of old Christmas supplies. Sniffed at it. Then looked up to Cassandra and Rayce. Its next *meow* sounded insistent.

"I think it's okay," Cassandra said. "Seems to be walking on all fours without trouble."

Rayce let out a heavy exhale and his embrace loosened. "Whew! I didn't want you to get hurt."

"I'm okay, Rayce." She kissed him. "You made sure of that. I always feel safe in your arms."

She laughed a little because speaking her emotions surprised her and at the same time felt better than right—it felt…marvelous.

Rayce took a deep breath, and said, "Cassandra. Would you be my girlfriend?"

"Yes." She smiled.

"Yes?"

She nodded. "You need more than that?"

Meow!

He looked over her shoulder. "That darn cat is getting into the fallen—Cassandra, look!"

He took her hand and plunged to the floor over the tangle of lights. Cassandra plucked up the star made from twigs. A twist of silver tinsel had been twined around the sticks and glued here and there. And in the center was the photo of her and her mom.

"I can't believe it." She pressed the ornament to her heart. Tears spilled down her cheeks. "It's almost as if the cat led us here."

The cat, seemingly proud of its accomplishment, *meow*ed happily.

Cassandra had just been given a hug from Heaven by her mother.

The next morning after Rayce left for an appointment with a guest, Cassandra ordered a few things from a local craft shop. Later in the afternoon, using the delivered supplies, she put the finishing paint touches to an ornament. It had been years since she'd felt the crafty urge, but this had been necessity.

"A little odd looking, but it's the thought that counts. Right?" she said to herself.

Tucking the ornament in a box, she then picked up the star made of twigs and studied the photo of her and her mom. "Thanks for leading me to this, Mom. You've made this a perfect Christmas. And I think I can do the same for someone whose one wish is to have a home."

That evening the staff met in the lobby for Christmas carols and a festive Christmas cookie exchange with the guests. Heading toward the party, Cassandra could already hear the carols jingling down the hallway. The scent of cinnamon and pine enticed her further, and the jingle of bells brightened her smile.

She saw Rayce leaning against the reception desk, wearing a sweater emblazoned with the face of the kid who had been left home alone, palms to his cheeks as he realized his situation. She gestured and got his attention. He beamed at the sight of her. As did her heart.

He strolled over and she tugged him around the corner away from the crowd.

"What's up, Snow Princess? I figured you'd get into all the singing and merrymaking."

"I do. Does that comment mean you don't?"

He shrugged. "It looks like fun, but I don't have any cookies for the exchange. Feels wrong to participate."

"Oh, please, Anita brings enough for everyone. Besides, you're the little drummer boy. You bring your charm and kindness to the event. It's your talent."

"Really?" He shrugged sheepishly. "I can work with that."

"I love the sweater. You never did tell me where you found that figurine."

"Eh. It's sort of a good luck charm I've carried with me through the years. Along with the drummer boy."

"I know you claimed the drummer boy after you gave it to me. You can have Kevin back, too, if you want him."

"How about we share them?"

"I like that. I seem to recall Kevin got a happily-ever-after ending?"

"He did. His family returned and he was once again safe in his home." Rayce sighed. "Corny, but it gets me every time."

"You'll find your home one of these days," she encouraged.

"I know I will. Did you bring the ornament to hang on the tree?"

"Of course." She showed him the star. "But first." She handed him the small box. "I have an ornament for you. You can hang it on the tree or keep it for your own tree."

"I've never had a tree..." He accepted the box.

"Someday you will."

He kissed her. "I love you, Snow Princess."

The announcement landed in her heart like the warmest winter kiss. True words, spoken clearly and with meaning. They echoed her own heartfelt beliefs. Cassandra nodded eagerly. "I love you, too."

For a moment the two held each other's gazes, their smiles growing. Love zinged back and forth between their eyes, their smiling mouths, their beating hearts. A kiss was necessary. Slow, soft and sweet. Didn't matter if the crowd witnessed this wondrous sign of affection. This was their marvelous kiss. No mistletoe required.

After a sigh and a bow of his forehead to hers, Rayce jiggled the box she'd given him. "So what do we have here?" He pulled out the tiny resin model of the Cobalt Lake Resort that they sold in the gift shop.

Before his smile dropped, Cassandra rushed to point out the detail she'd added. "It's our resort, but look there. The little man standing in the front?"

He studied it curiously. "Oh, yeah. He's wearing a green jacket."

"That's you! I painted the figure. Rayce, the resort is your home now."

He looked to her, his eyes going watery.

"You are always welcome here, in Whistler and…in my heart."

"I don't know what to say." He clutched the ornament against his chest. "It feels like a home. Especially when I'm with you. Thank you. This is the nicest gift I've ever been given."

She kissed him and then tapped his lips. "Oh, I've got a better one for you later. When we're in bed."

A single eyebrow zipped upward.

With dramatic flair, Cassandra pulled something out of her pants pocket and brandished it between them.

"Are you kidding me?" He studied the crumbled plastic mistletoe. "That thing has certainly gotten a lot of good use."

"Are you going to kiss me again or marvel over a silly piece of plastic?"

He didn't need any more motivation than her flutter of lashes.

"You've changed my life," he said after the kiss. "I love you."

"I'm so glad you came to Cobalt Lake Resort. You helped me to find a place in my heart for my mom's memory. And I have another place right here." She patted her chest.

"What's that for?"

"For you of course. You can stay there as long as you like."

"In that case me and my figurines are moving in."

"You'll all fit. My heart is your home." She tapped the ornament she'd made for him. "Shall we hang these on the tree?"

"Definitely."

They snuck in behind the guests who were singing in harmony to a Christmas song that Kathy played on her portable keyboard. Cookies were munched and hot chocolate sipped. Her dad, clad in an outrageous Christmas sweater decorated with tinsel and real flashing lights, stood across the room with an arm around Faith, who wore a matching sweater. He winked at her and nodded.

Lured by the twinkling lights on the Christmas tree, Cassandra led Rayce around to the front of it. He studied the pine boughs filled with tinsel and ornaments, and then hung his ornament in the front. "How's that?"

"I'll notice that little green jacket every time I walk by."

"You did get my charming good looks right." He tapped the tiny man. "Your turn," he said.

With a squeeze of his hand and a reassuring nod from him, Cassandra placed the star ornament front and center. Then she stepped back and into Rayce's arms. The place she felt most comfortable. And loved.

The memories she held of her mother were now safe in her heart. And this new memory of love and acceptance was exactly where it belonged. Now everything was...

"Marvelous," she announced.

EPILOGUE

ON BOXING DAY Cassandra glided slowly down the slope with Rayce by her side. She'd chosen a gentle run for her first time on skis in almost two years. But after a pep talk and a kiss from her boyfriend, confidence had flooded her system. And she felt sure her mom was watching her from above. Another star in the sky twinkling next to Rayce's grandparents.

Rayce skied closer and reached for her hand. "You're doing it, Snow Princess!"

"I am! I missed this so much!"

"Let's ski together every day," he said.

"Works for me!"

They neared the bottom of the slope and with a twist of her hips Cassandra came to a stop, followed by Rayce. He tugged off his gloves and leaned over to kiss her. His wink sparkled brighter than her heart. Oh, she'd been captured by his eyes. And his incredibly smart heart.

"I have a crazy idea," he said.

"Does it involve more cat-wrangling?"

"Hey, Caspar adopted me after the incident in the shed. He won't leave my cabin. I know it's because of my handsome good looks."

"Naturally. It couldn't be anything but." How she adored his self-effacing slips into ego. It was who he was, and she wouldn't wish him to change.

"But taking in a stray cat is not the crazy idea."

"Do tell?"

He took her hand and bowed his forehead to hers. Standing there for a moment, they shared the quiet stillness of the crisp winter day. And when Cassandra started to ask about his idea, he suddenly kissed her forehead and asked, "Do you want to look for a house together in Whistler?"

The question didn't even startle her. In fact it felt like the perfect next step in her dream that had come true.

"You mean a *home*?" she asked.

His smile beamed. "Most definitely. A home."

* * * * *

HARLEQUIN
Reader Service

Enjoyed your book?

Try the perfect subscription for Romance readers and get more great books like this delivered right to your door.

See why over 10+ million readers have tried Harlequin Reader Service.

Start with a Free Welcome Collection with free books and a gift—valued over $20.

Choose any series in print or ebook.
See website for details and order today:

   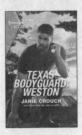

TryReaderService.com/subscriptions